"You don't think you're going to spend the night here?"

"And tomorrow night, and the night after. I'm moving in, Faye."

"Over my dead body!" she said explosively.

While she stared at him, speechless, he opened the front door and began carrying in his bags that were piled up outside.

"No!" she cried. "This is my home. I won't have you walking in here without a by-your-leave."

She stopped at the sound of feet pattering in from the kitchen. The next moment her little daughter was standing in the doorway, a look of ecstasy dawning on her face. Cindy drew a deep, thrilled breath, shrieked "Daddy!" and hurled herself into his arms.

Cindy nodded vigorously, beaming. A growing under-

Dear Reader,

Welcome to

Everyone has special occasions in their life—times of celebration and excitement. Maybe it's a romantic event, an engagement or a wedding—or perhaps a wonderful family occasion, such as the birth of a baby. Or even a personal milestone—a thirtieth or fortieth birthday!

These are all important times in our lives and in **The Big Event!** you can see how different couples react to these events. Whatever the occasion, romance and drama are guaranteed!

We've been featuring some terrific stories from some of your favorite authors. If you've enjoyed this miniseries so far, next month go to your bookstore and look for the Harlequin Presents® shelf. There you'll find another title in **The Big Event!**—*Bride for a Year* by Katherine Ross—which guarantees excitement and passion. Will a husband and wife face divorce or will they get to celebrate their first wedding anniversary?

Happy Reading!

The Editors

The Diamond Dad
Lucy Gordon

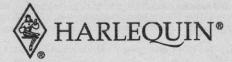

HARLEQUIN®

TORONTO • NEW YORK • LONDON
AMSTERDAM • PARIS • SYDNEY • HAMBURG
STOCKHOLM • ATHENS • TOKYO • MILAN • MADRID
PRAGUE • WARSAW • BUDAPEST • AUCKLAND

ISBN 0-373-03515-2

THE DIAMOND DAD

First North American Publication 1998.

Printed in U.S.A.

CHAPTER ONE

'*You!*' Garth Clayton said in a stunned voice. 'What are you doing here?'

Faye, his estranged wife, faced him with her head up. Inwardly she was thinking, Two years, and he still hasn't forgiven me! Will that make it easier, or harder, to do what I have to?

'Aren't you going to invite me in?' she asked.

He didn't move. 'When you left this house you swore that you'd never come back.'

'We both said a lot of angry things on that night, but we didn't mean them.'

'I meant every word,' he said, unyielding.

He seemed older than his thirty-five years, she thought. There was a new darkness in his brown eyes and fine lines at the corners that hadn't been there before. He looked as though he lived on his nerves, neither eating nor sleeping enough. But he would always be a tall, handsome man, whose sensual, mobile mouth had once thrilled her, even though that mouth now had a look of strain and bitterness.

Faye knew that she, too, had altered. The gauche teenager of their wedding day had become a mother of two children with a mind of her own and enough strength to stand up to her husband's forceful personality. These days she had a poise and confidence that was reflected in the strong colours she wore, replacing the delicate hues of a few years ago.

'I've come to talk,' she said.

He stood back to let her pass. She could feel his eyes on her, taking in the new short crop of her light brown hair. She wasn't expensively dressed, but she had a tall, slender figure that made everything look good. Her russet suit with its gilt buttons looked stylish, suggesting a woman who was at ease with herself.

He indicated the living room and Faye was a little surprised to find it just as she remembered. Garth had been so angry when she left that she'd pictured him wiping out all traces of her, but everything was the same. This was where they'd had their final quarrel, when she'd tried vainly to make him understand why she had to escape him.

'A drink?' he asked.

'No thank you. I'm driving.'

His eyebrows raised a little. 'You've learned to drive?'

'Yes, I found it quite easy.'

'When you had an instructor who could keep calm,' he finished wryly.

'That helped,' she admitted.

Their very first vehicle had been a shabby third-hand truck to get Garth started as a builder. Later, when the money had flowed freely, he'd bought her an expensive car and had tried to teach her to drive, but it had been a disaster. She'd lacked the confidence to try again, and when she fled she'd left the car behind.

Disturbing feelings began to play back. Perhaps she shouldn't have come to this luxurious house, which he'd built 'for her' but which reflected his own tastes. Here, she'd shared a bed with Garth but nothing else, and she'd always disliked the place. Yet she'd smothered her true feelings, as so often in her marriage, and pretended delight to please her husband.

That, however, was in the past. Their marriage was over in all but name. She was her own woman now.

Once her heart had beat with eager anticipation at the thought of seeing Garth Clayton. With his dark hair, vivid looks and lithe grace, he'd seemed almost godlike to the eighteen-year-old Faye. He'd worked on a building site that she'd passed every day on her way to work in a dress shop. Sometimes she would stop and regard him from a distance, admiring the way he leaped over the scaffolding, never afraid of the drop, or lifted heavy weights as though they were nothing.

She was so innocent that she hardly recognized her admiration for his splendid body as the flickering of desire. She only knew that she *had* to make him notice her. When at last he winked at her, she blushed deeply and scurried away to the shop. For the rest of the day she was nearly useless, having to be recalled from a trance when someone spoke to her, and giving customers the wrong change. Her boss spoke sharply, but Faye barely heard. She was in seventh heaven.

He was waiting for her at the wire next morning. 'Didn't mean to upset you yesterday,' he said gruffly.

'You didn't. I was just—surprised.'

'Surprised? A pretty girl like you?'

Bliss! He'd called her pretty.

They went to the cinema but to her disappointment he didn't kiss her, only brushed her hand against his cheek. She was wretched, sure that he found her boring. But he asked her out again, and on the third date he kissed her. She thought there couldn't be more happiness than that in the world.

But there was. The memory of their first lovemaking could still bring tears to her eyes. The young Garth had vigour rather than subtlety but he was kind and gentle, treating her as something precious.

'Don't go yet,' he begged as she got dressed.

'I have to. I'll miss my last bus.'

'I'll come home with you. I don't want to say goodbye.'

'But there's no bus back,' she said, loving him for not wanting to say goodbye.

In the end he came to the stop with her and held her close until the bus appeared. She sat at the back so that she could watch him standing in the road with his hands stretched up to the glass. And when the bus moved off he stayed there, his eyes fixed on her until she turned the corner.

When they weren't making love, they talked. He told her how he dreamed of being his own boss, a builder with a little business that would grow. For him, the sky was the limit. Faye couldn't remember discussing what she wanted from life. But then, all she wanted was him.

When she told him she was pregnant he said, 'I've got a week free between jobs next month. We'll use that for our honeymoon.'

'Honeymoon?' she echoed joyfully. 'You mean—get married?'

'Of *course* we're going to get married!'

She was too happy to care that he told her, not asked her. She wanted to be his wife more than anything in the world. They were married in a register office and spent a week by the sea in a borrowed caravan that had seen better days. With almost no money, there was little to do except walk hand in hand on the beach, eat whatever was cheap, and love, and love, and love. It was a time of unspoiled bliss and she was sure that their marriage would be a success.

But that was when she was an innocent who believed love was for ever, before the discovery of Garth's true character and the gradual destruction of all that gave her happiness. Now they'd reached the end of the road, and she'd come driving through the darkness to Elm Ridge to confront him.

He followed her into the living room and stood waiting for her to begin. The air was alive with tension and she knew this was going to be harder than she'd thought. To give herself a moment she slipped off her jacket, revealing a sleeveless olive-green shirt, adorned by a chain.

Garth studied that chain. Solid gold if he was any judge. Simple, yet very costly. Not something she would have bought for herself, nor one of his own gifts, most of which she'd left behind.

Her perfume was elusive, like woodsmoke drifting on the breeze. It had a subtlety that told him more clearly than anything else that he no longer knew this woman.

'You sure picked your moment to come calling,' he said. 'I was about to go to bed.'

'I left it late to give you time to get home from work. I hope I haven't interrupted you when you have company.'

'A woman? No, that was one accusation even you were never able to throw at me, although apparently I was every other kind of villain.'

'I never said that, Garth. It was just that I couldn't live with you any more.'

'So you claimed. I never quite understood why.'

'I tried to explain—'

'I gather that my crime was to work day and night to give you a comfortable life, with every luxury you could want. For this I was punished by the loss of my wife and both my children.' A touch of iron in his voice made it clear that he was as unyielding as ever.

'Perhaps I'd better go away and return another time…'

'No! You must have come here for some reason. You've kept well clear of me, Faye. Even when the children visit me, you never come with them. When I collect them from your house, you speak to me as little as possible.'

'I don't want to upset them with fighting.'

'How are they? It seems a long time since I saw them.'

'You could have seen them last week if you'd come to Cindy's school play, as you promised. She had the lead. She was longing for you to be there and be proud of her.'

'I meant to, but at the last minute something came up.'

Faye sighed. 'Something always did come up, Garth. A business deal was always more important than your children.'

'That's not true. I was there for Adrian's birthday.'

'Only for two hours. And you didn't come to see him playing football, did you? He really minded about that. And Cindy was heartbroken when you missed her birthday last year. She loves you so much, and you let her down all the time. It's her birthday again next week. She'll be eight. Oh please, Garth, try to be there, just this once.'

'Saturday? Hell, I don't think I can make it. I've got a client—' He saw her looking at him with resignation and said, 'Was this what you came for?'

'No, I came to say I want a divorce.'

He took a sharp breath. 'That's a bit sudden, isn't it?'

'We've been separated for two years. You've always known I wanted a divorce.'

'I thought you'd have seen sense by now.'

'You mean, return to you?' She gave a brief, wry laugh. 'I remember that your version of seeing sense was always people doing what suited you.'

'Because I was the reasonable one! Look at how you behaved after you left. It was always crazy for you to live in that poky little house while I was alone in this huge place. You could have a beautiful home but you prefer a rabbit hutch. You wouldn't even let me give you enough money for a decent place.'

'You pay to support the children—'

'But you won't accept a penny for yourself,' he said bitterly. 'Do you know how that makes me feel?'

'I'm sorry, Garth, but I don't want to depend on you. That puzzles you, doesn't it? Your life is dedicated to squeezing the last penny out of every deal. You don't understand someone who doesn't want money from you, but I don't. I never did. I wanted—' She checked herself.

'What, Faye? What did you want? Because I swear I never found out what it was.'

'Didn't you? And yet at one time you gave it to me,' she said with a touch of wistfulness. 'When we were first married, everything I needed came from you. On our wedding day I was the happiest woman on earth. I had your love; I was expecting our baby—'

'We rented a two-roomed flat with no hot water,' he recalled.

'I didn't care. All I cared about was loving you, and having you love me.'

'Did I ever stop?' he demanded. 'Was there one day of our marriage when I wasn't trying to give you the best of everything? I did it all to please you, and you tossed it back at me like so much garbage.'

'I already had the best of everything. But you took it away.'

'I didn't stop loving you,' he said almost angrily.

'But you stopped having time for me.'

He would have answered, but the phone began to ring. He snatched up the receiver. 'I'll get rid of whoever it is. Hello— Look, I can't talk now, I'm tied up— Oh, hell! Can't he call back later?— I know I've been trying to get him, but— All right! Put him through.'

'I see your technique for getting rid of people hasn't improved,' Faye said lightly.

He scowled. 'Five minutes. That's all. I'll take it in the study.'

'Can I make myself some tea?'

'This is your home. Go where you like!' He vanished into the study.

The big, glamorous kitchen had all the latest gadgetry cunningly concealed beneath oak and copper pots. That and the dark red tiles on the floor gave it an air of warmth, but Faye had never found it warm. Garth had told her to select whatever decor she liked, but then promoted his own preference so insistently that she'd yielded. It seemed to have been chosen not for herself, but for someone called Garth Clayton's wife. Was it then she'd started to feel that she didn't fit the role? No, much earlier.

How eagerly he'd first shown her the house! It was set in its own grounds on a slight incline, surrounded by elm trees. 'Here you are, darling,' he'd said. 'Welcome to Elm Ridge. Your new home, like you always wanted.' His pride had been touching, and she'd lacked the heart to say that it wasn't the home she'd wanted. Nothing like it.

Her dream home had been 'a little place all our own', as he'd once promised. And two years after their marriage they'd had a small house, for Garth was a man born to succeed. She'd been completely happy. But four years later he'd swept her away into this big, unfriendly mansion. She'd even had a housekeeper, a bustling, kindly soul called Nancy. Faye made friends with her and enjoyed many a chat in the kitchen, for she felt more at home with Nancy than with any of her husband's new, moneyed friends.

When the tea was made she wandered back to the study door, behind which she could hear him arguing with someone. Long experience made her murmur, 'Half an hour at the least.'

Wherever she looked she could see few changes. The pictures on the stair walls were the ones she'd chosen. She'd taken one of them with her, and its place was still blank.

Here she'd once been unhappy and stifled. Garth had been generous, giving her everything that money could buy, but he'd also arranged her life and their children's lives, from on high. The little builder's yard he'd managed to scrape together had nearly gone under in the first year. He'd saved it by the skin of his teeth, but Faye had known nothing about this until she'd learned by accident three years later. The discovery that she'd been excluded from his inner counsels had been like a blow over the heart.

He'd failed to see that she was no longer the blindly adoring girl he'd married. She'd matured into a woman with a mind of her own, who still loved him, but now knew that he wasn't perfect.

They argued about the children. Garth was pleased with his son yet hardly seemed to notice his daughter. But Cindy adored her father and Faye often saw a wistful look in the child's eyes at his neglect.

Adrian, too, suffered a kind of neglect. Garth would buy him anything, but he wouldn't take time off to watch Adrian play in the school football team. He was determined to rear the boy to be 'successful' as he understood the word, but Adrian wanted to be a footballer. Garth dismissed this with a shrug. 'He'll grow out of it,' he told Faye. 'Just don't encourage him.'

She yielded in their disputes, telling herself that to be with him was enough. But her children were another matter. She stood up for them with a strength that surprised Garth. Arguments became quarrels. When she could stand it no longer, she left him, taking the children.

The last thing he said to her was 'Don't fool yourself that it's over, Faye. It never will be.'

She continued upstairs, to what had been Adrian's room, but the door was locked. So was Cindy's, and the one that led into the bedroom she'd shared with Garth. Frowning, she returned downstairs.

Here the doors were open and next to the study Faye found Garth's new bedroom, little more than a monkish cupboard, with a plain bed and a set of mahogany furniture. The walls were white; the carpet biscuit-coloured. Everything was of excellent quality but the total effect was bleak, as though the man who owned it carried bleakness within himself.

The sole ornament was a photograph beside the bed, showing a young boy of about nine, with a bright, eager face. Faye smiled, recognizing Adrian, but her smile changed to a frown as she saw there was no picture of Cindy.

She waited in the hall until he emerged from the study.

'What's the matter?' he asked, seeing her face.

'I'd like to see your study. There's something I have to know.'

The study told her the same story. There on the desk were two photographs of Adrian, but none of Cindy.

'How dare you?' she said, turning on him. 'You had no right to censor your own child out of existence. Cindy's still your daughter, and she loves you.'

'I don't know what you—'

'Where's her picture? You've got Adrian's. Where's Cindy's?'

'Look, I'm sorry. I didn't do it on purpose. I just didn't notice—'

'You never noticed her, and you broke her heart. The only one you cared for was Adrian, and then only when you could see yourself in him. But he isn't like you. He's gentle and sensitive.'

'There's nothing gentle about him when he's kicking a ball around a pitch.'

'How would you know? You've hardly ever seen him. Yes, he plays a tough game but he's a nice person. He looks after Cindy; he cares about people.'

'Everything I'm not, apparently,' he said in a tight voice.

'Yes. He doesn't like the things you like, and I won't have him forced to be someone he isn't. That's one of the reasons I left: to protect them from you.'

'That's a dreadful thing to say,' he told her, his face very pale.

'It's a dreadful thing to be true. Garth, I came here tonight because I'm tired of living in limbo. I really want that divorce.'

'I'll never give you one. I told you that when you left.'

'Yes, you said you'd take the children if I went for a divorce. That scared me at the time. You even used it to make me give up my job—'

'You didn't need to work. I offered you a large allowance—'

'But I wanted to be independent.'

He didn't understand that. He never had. He'd thought it madness when she'd struggled to get a diploma in bookkeeping through a correspondence course. She'd been thrilled to get work with Kendall Haines, a local environmentalist, but Garth's bitter anger had made her leave the job.

Refusing to be defeated, she'd approached the problem in a different way. She had a real flair for bookkeeping and began taking in freelance work from several small, local businesses. She'd used a computer that had been very basic even when she'd bought it second-hand, and which now looked as if it had come out of the Ark. The budget wouldn't run to the modern machine she longed for, yet still she was content. She'd won her independence in the face of Garth's hostility.

But his high-handed action still rankled. 'I was happy in that job until you forced me to leave it to stop you claiming Cindy and Adrian,' she told him now. 'I couldn't see it then, but that threat was nonsense. No court would have given you the children, and if it had you wouldn't have known what to do with them. It's just that you can't bear to let go of what was once yours. But we're not property, and it's time to let go.'

'What makes you think I've changed my mind?'

'It doesn't matter. Time has passed. Sooner or later we'll divorce, and I'd like it to be sooner. Our tenth wedding anniversary is coming up, and I don't want to be legally your wife on that day. Can't you see that it would be a mockery?'

'You were still my wife on our ninth anniversary. What difference does it make now?'

'The tenth is special,' she argued. 'It's the first of the big ones: ten, twenty, twenty-five, fifty. Ten is like a milestone. It says that your marriage has lasted. But ours hasn't.'

He looked at her closely. 'Is that the only reason?'

Under his keen gaze, she coloured. 'No, I—I want to get married again.'

She waited for his anger at this offence to his pride, but it didn't come and this disconcerted her. 'Tell me about him,' he said mildly.

'He's a kind man and I love him.'

'And you think he can fill my place with my children?'

'He already does and he's doing a terrific job. He's *there* for them.'

'He has no right to be. I'm still their father, just as I'm still your husband.'

'And what you have, you hold. I might have known.'

He touched the gold chain about her neck. 'Did he give you this?'

'Yes.'

'I wouldn't have thought Kendall Haines could have afforded that. He's obviously more successful than I realized. But he still isn't the right man for you.'

'I never told you his name. How did you—?' She gasped in outrage. *'You've had me spied on!'*

'I always keep up-to-date information about my investments,' he said coolly. 'I knew when you went to work for him, and the first time you dated him.'

She drew a sharp breath. 'That was why you made me leave that job,' she said angrily. 'Because I was falling in love with him. You're even trying to control me now.'

'This man isn't right for you.'

'I think he is and I'm going to marry him. I can't be browbeaten any more, Garth—'

He took a quick breath. 'Browbeaten? Is that how you think of a marriage in which I gave you everything—?'

'Except yourself. Once you got your own business you were never there when I needed you. You handed your gifts down from on high and expected me to defer to you, and when I started answering back you didn't like it. I had to escape—'

'You'll never escape me,' he said harshly. 'I won't allow it.'

'You think you're going to turn the full might of the law onto me—?'

'No, it's much simpler than that,' he said softly, and pulled her into his arms.

He was too quick for her to avoid him and before she knew it his lips were on hers, caressing her with the same fierce purpose as in the past. In the beginning it had delighted her. Now, she was filled with outrage at his arrogance. Once, their sexual rapport had been perfect. Even when they had quarrelled it had still been there, giving them an illusion of a marriage. Now he thought he had only to remind her of that to overcome her will.

She fought to remain still and inwardly resist him. It should be easy with her anger to help her. Besides, she was strong now. If she waited, he would soon see that it was no use.

But his lips were full of persuasion, coaxing her to

relive hot, brilliant moments, when the world had been full of love and beauty. If he'd been possessive, so had she, caressing and cherishing his body, rejoicing that he had chosen her for this magic gift. He had been young and his frame had been at its magnificent best; long legs and arms, a smooth brown chest, and hips whose power could make her cry out with ecstasy.

In the lonely, sobbing nights after their separation, she'd fought to deaden those memories and believed she'd succeeded. But he was here now, the living, breathing man, determined to make her remember what had united them, and forget what had driven them apart.

'You'll never escape me,' he murmured against her mouth, 'as long as we have *this*.'

His lips moved insistently against hers. This. One little word to sum up a dazzling, glorious and finally bitter experience: passion and grief intermingled. Love, pain, disillusion. All these things were there the moment he touched her, indestructible after all this time.

'I never forgot you,' he said hoarsely. 'Not for a moment. You were always with me—just as I was always with you—'

She tried to deny it but the treacherous warmth was already filling her body, weakening her will, making her want things she had no right to want. She'd sworn this wouldn't happen, but the memory of his passion still lived in her flesh, recalling her to life. She had once loved him so much, and though love might be finished, she was what that love had made her, and the past could never be destroyed completely.

For a few treacherous moments her body moulded itself to his, burning with remembered desire and need. She'd belonged to him completely, but that was a long time ago—although it seemed only yesterday—this very moment—for ever—

'It's not so easy, is it, Faye?' he whispered. 'It's not so easy to forget the truth…'

But the arrogant words shouted in her brain like a warning. Faye shuddered as she saw how close she'd come to weakening. Garth was a clever man and this was no more than a cynical mockery of love. She took a deep breath and forced her head to clear.

'The truth is that everything is over between us,' she said emphatically. 'Can't you understand that?'

'Why should I?' he growled. 'You don't kiss me as though it was all over.'

'I'm in love with another man…'

'Little liar!'

'And I'm going to marry him. You can't stop me.' Putting out all her strength, she broke free of him. 'You thought it was going to be easy, didn't you, Garth? When I arrived tonight you were sure I was going to drop into your hands. But I'm not like that any more. I've made my own life and there's no room in it for you.'

Garth was very pale. 'We'll see about that.'

But he was talking to empty air. Faye had fled the house.

CHAPTER TWO

'FAYE, you shouldn't have been alone with this man. He's a monster.'

Faye smiled at Kendall Haines, the man she planned to marry as soon as she was free. 'Garth isn't a monster,' she protested. 'He just steamrollers over people.'

'All the more reason for you to stay away from him.'

It was the day after Faye's visit, and she and Kendall were spending the afternoon together at her home. It was as small and modest as Elm Ridge was rich and grand, but it was her very own and she loved it. The furniture was mostly second-hand, and it showed the wear and tear of two boisterous children. The house looked what it was, a place where a family lived, a real home.

Faye was dressed to fit in with the furniture, in a worn pair of jeans, topped off by a flowered shirt.

Kendall's voice became firm. 'You must promise never to do such a thing again. I can't bear to think that you're still legally his wife.'

'Not for much longer.'

Faye plumped up the cushions as she spoke so as not to let him see her face. There were things about her meeting with Garth she couldn't speak of. She was still shocked at the treacherous way her body had responded to him at the very moment she was rejecting him.

'Do you mean that he's actually agreed to a divorce?' Kendall demanded.

'Not exactly...'

'Then he's still fighting you.'

'It doesn't matter,' Faye said with a conviction she was far from feeling. 'When we broke up he threatened to claim custody of the children if I insisted on a divorce, so I didn't. But after all this time, he hasn't any cards to play.'

'It's time I went to see him,' Kendall mused.

'Ken, no. Don't even think of it.'

'But you're not handling him very well, and perhaps some straight talking would do the trick.'

Kendall believed in straight talking. He was a vet and a minor celebrity in the ecological world. Occasionally he was invited onto television panels, where his forthright manner went down well.

'Straight talking is the worst thing with Garth,' Faye protested. 'He can talk back even straighter.'

'You think I can't handle him?' he asked, raising his eyebrows in amusement.

She could understand his confidence. There was a massiveness about Kendall, both in his physique and his personality. He was six foot two, broad-shouldered, with copper hair that touched his collar, and a beard. He sometimes resembled a lion.

But if Kendall was a lion, Faye thought, Garth was a panther, ready to spring and demolish unwary prey.

'Ken, please, forget this idea,' she begged. 'It would only make things worse.'

His mouth tightened slightly in displeasure. Then he shrugged, good humour restored, and drew her close for a kiss. But they jumped apart almost at once as the front door banged and there came the sound of children's voices. Faye sat up hastily, straightening her hair just in time.

Two attractive children, both dressed in jeans and trainers, bounced into the room and greeted Kendall.

Cindy, almost eight, had the dark hair and intense eyes of her father. Nine-year-old Adrian had his mother's fairness, her fine features, and her sensitivity. He and Kendall grinned at each other. Cindy regarded her mother's friend with more reserve but still offered him a toffee, which he accepted at once for he had a very sweet tooth.

'Tea will be ready in ten minutes,' Faye said, hugging her. 'Go and have some sort of wash.'

Both children made ritual groaning noises, but headed for the door. Adrian turned back to Kendall. 'You will play football with me before you go, won't you?'

'Promise.'

Adrian vanished, satisfied.

'Do we have to jump apart like a pair of canoodling teenagers?' Kendall asked plaintively. 'The kids know about us. They even like me.'

'Adrian especially,' Faye agreed. 'But Cindy still adores Garth. That's why we have his picture over there. It's part of her make-believe that one day things will come right. I get so angry that he doesn't treasure her picture in the same way.'

'Don't let him get to you,' Kendall said with a shrug.

'You're right. He's the past.' She put her arms about him. 'Once I've got this divorce, everything will be fine for us.'

For three days Faye waited to hear from Garth, but there wasn't a word. Reluctantly she decided that she would have to contact him again, but just now she was snowed under with work.

She was settling down to it one afternoon when a sound outside drew her attention, and she was surprised to see a luxurious black car drawing up outside. The next

moment Garth stepped out and headed purposefully towards the house.

Faye pulled open the door. 'I wasn't expecting you,'
she said.

'I only decided this morning. May I come in?' The
question was a formality, as he'd already taken her
shoulders and moved her gently but firmly out of his
way.

She concealed her annoyance at his high-handedness,
thinking that perhaps he'd come about the divorce.

'You left this behind,' he said, handing her a parcel.
Inside, she found the jacket that she had left behind in
her hurry to escape from Elm Ridge. It startled her
slightly to realize that she hadn't even thought about it.

'Thank you,' she said awkwardly. 'It was good of you
to bring it yourself—'

'I wanted to talk to you. We can't leave things as they
are. Are the kids here?'

'No, they're out with Kendall.'

'He's really taken over, hasn't he?'

'He's my future husband. Of course he's getting to
know them. They like him a lot. Please, don't let's have
a fight about him.'

'All right. I haven't come to fight. Do I get offered a
cup of coffee?'

Reluctantly Faye went into the kitchen but she was
very aware of him studying the house, the inside of
which he'd never seen before. When he'd collected his
children for a visit he'd waited outside, or even sent the
car with only his chauffeur.

She came into the front room with the tray, to find
him studying her computer and the papers strewn on the
table.

'What's this?' he asked critically.

'It's my job.'

'You're still working?'

'Didn't your spies tell you? You drove me out of Kendall's job, but you couldn't stop me doing freelance work.' She was struck by a horrid thought and hastily shut down the file she was working on.

'Don't worry, I'm not going to twist anyone's arm to make them fire you,' he said with a wry smile.

'I wouldn't put it past you.'

'Forget it. That's not what I'm here for.'

'What *are* you here for?'

'Because I'm tired of waiting. It's over, Faye. All this living in limbo has gone on long enough. It's time to make final decisions.'

'That's what I was trying to tell you the other night.'

'But we got distracted, didn't we?' he reminded her with a wicked grin.

To her own annoyance Faye found herself blushing. 'That won't happen again. I've made my decision, and in future I think we should talk through lawyers.'

'Faye, if you've become as strong and independent as you claim, why don't you deal with your problems, instead of running away from them?'

'What do you mean by that?' she demanded angrily.

'If I'm a problem, deal with me. Here I am. Confront me. Make me back down.'

'You'd love me to try, so that you could make a show of strength, wouldn't you? You fight your way; I'll fight mine. I don't need to confront you to make you back down over this divorce. I think you should go now. Please tell your driver to— Where is he? Your car's gone.'

'I told him not to stay.'

'When is he coming back for you?'

'Tomorrow morning.'

'You don't think you're going to spend the night here?'

'And tomorrow night, and the night after. I'm moving in, Faye.'

'Over my dead body!' she said explosively.

'It's time I studied the influences my children are receiving.'

While she stared at him, speechless, he opened the front door and began carrying in his bags that were piled up just outside.

'No!' she cried. 'This is my home. I won't have you walking in here without a by-your-leave.'

'We need to be under the same roof for a while. If you don't want me here, come back to Elm Ridge.'

'That's out of the question!'

'Then it'll have to be here.'

'There's no room for you. We only have three bedrooms. One for Adrian, one for Cindy and one for me.'

'We can work something out.'

She was distracted by the sight of Kendall's car drawing up outside. The last thing she wanted was for the two men to meet now. Luckily Kendall was in a hurry. Having watched until the children reached the house, he waved and drove off.

Adrian came in first. 'Cindy's gone round the back,' he told Faye. 'She's got dirty shoes.' His eager look faded as he saw his father, and he edged closer to Faye.

Watching their faces, Faye followed both their reactions easily. She saw Garth wait for his son's whoop of delight, then grow tense when it didn't come. Adrian seemed uncertain. In Kendall he'd found a fellow-footballer, who sympathized with him as Garth never had. Yet he loved and admired his father, and she could see that he was torn between the two loyalties.

'Hello, Daddy,' he said at last. 'What are you—? I mean— Has something happened?'

'I've come to stay for a while,' Garth said, pretending not to notice his son's awkwardness.

'Oh. That's nice.'

'Is that all you've got to say to me, son?' Garth asked, with determined cheerfulness. 'Doesn't your old man get a hug?'

Adrian hugged him obediently. Faye came to the child's rescue. 'Go and change those dirty clothes,' she said with a smile.

He turned to her with relief. 'We had ever such a good time, Mummy. I found a frog.'

'Yuk! You didn't bring it home, I hope.'

'No, I wanted to, but Ken said it would be happier where it was.'

'Thank goodness one of you's got some sense. Off now.'

When the boy had gone Faye saw the condemnation in Garth's eyes. 'I thought he at least would be pleased to see me,' he said bitterly. 'Your boyfriend's done his best to distance my son from me, hasn't he?'

'No, you did that. Ken's simply given him all the attention you never did. He's taken trouble to know who Adrian really is.'

'Evidently I'm here not a moment too soon.'

'Garth, about your staying—'

She stopped at the sound of feet pattering in from the kitchen. Next moment her little daughter was standing in the doorway, a look of ecstasy dawning on her face. Cindy drew a deep, thrilled breath, shrieked, *'Daddy!'* and hurled herself into his arms.

Garth reeled under the impact, then lifted her high off the ground so that she could hug him properly. Two strong young arms tightened around his neck so firmly that he was almost strangled, but he clung on to the one person who was pleased to see him.

'Daddy, Daddy, Daddy…' Cindy squealed in delight.

'Steady, pet,' he said in a choked voice. 'I can't breathe.' He set her down and knelt to meet her eyes. 'Let me look at you. It's been a long ti— That is—er— let me have a good look at you.' He was struggling for the right words. What did you say to a little girl whom you hardly knew? But she made it easy for him, bouncing up and down, hugging and kissing him.

'You came back,' she bubbled. 'You remembered my birthday. You did, you did, you did!'

With a shock Garth's eyes met Faye's. He hadn't remembered Cindy's birthday, and even now he couldn't recall the exact date.

'Mummy said not to be disappointed if you forgot,' Cindy said. 'But I *knew* you wouldn't.'

He had the grace to be conscience-stricken. 'Of course I didn't forget,' he improvised. Frantically his eyes meet Faye's, asking her help.

'Daddy knows it's your birthday on Saturday,' she said. 'In fact he came over to tell us that he'll be spending the whole day with us.'

Cindy squealed again with delight. Garth ground his teeth at the way Faye had backed him into a corner. Saturday was fully booked with important meetings. Faye's eyes were still on him, understanding everything, daring him to refuse.

He thought faster than he'd ever done in his life. 'That's right,' he said. 'We'll all be going out together. You, me, Mummy and Adrian.'

'Adrian's got a football match that afternoon,' Cindy said. 'Can we all go and watch it?'

'Of course we will,' Garth responded at once. 'Actually, I thought of inviting myself to stay with you for a while. Only if you want me, of course.' He was throwing the challenge back at Faye.

'Of *course* we want you,' Cindy declared, shocked. 'We do, don't we, Mummy? We want Daddy ever and *ever* so much.'

'Well, it's not quite that simple,' Garth said, as if giving the matter serious thought. 'You see, this house has only three bedrooms, so there isn't anywhere for me.'

'But it's easy,' Cindy said. 'I'll move in with Mummy and you can have my room.'

'Can I, darling? That's very nice of you.' He looked at Faye. 'You see? It's easy.'

Cindy danced off to find her brother, singing, 'Daddy's home! Daddy's home!' The other two regarded each other.

'I think you're the most unscrupulous man I've ever known,' Faye seethed. 'How dare you use a child's love in that cynical way?'

'But perhaps I'm not being cynical, Faye. You told me I should pay them more attention, especially Cindy. That's what I'm doing. Don't you think I've made her happy?'

'For your own ends, the way everything is for your own ends.'

'She's *happy*. Does it matter why?'

'It *will* matter, when you decide to change tactics and drop her. It's bad enough that you've neglected her until now, but when she finds that this sudden interest is only a way of using her, she'll stop trusting you. I don't want her to lose faith in the world so soon.'

'Would I do that to my own child?'

'You wouldn't even know you were doing it,' she said despairingly. 'But you mustn't do this. Go away, Garth. Leave us alone. We were happy without you—'

'Was Cindy?'

'All right, we weren't happy, but we survived.'

'And you don't think you could be happy with me around?'

'I don't think anyone could be happy with you around,' she said desperately. 'You don't bring happiness, or know how to create it. You only know *things*. Getting them, winning them, and buying them. Go back to that. You're good at it. But with people, you only destroy…'

Her voice choked off, and she turned sharply away.

'What is it?' Garth asked, coming after her.

'Nothing!'

'You're not crying, are you?'

'No, I'm not crying,' she insisted, quickly brushing her eyes. For a moment she'd been shaken by the thought of Garth here, ruining her hard-won peace. But she definitely wasn't crying.

'Here, let me look at you,' he said, turning her to face him. He pulled a clean handkerchief from his pocket and dabbed her eyes. 'There's no need to get upset about this.' His voice softened. 'I'm not really so bad, Faye.'

'Yes, you are,' she said huskily, almost hating him for that gentle note. She could cope with him angry, but gentleness recalled too many sweet memories that she had to block out to survive.

'Then teach me to be better. While I'm here you can show me how to get closer to the children, the way you've always said I should.'

'You're not going to stay here,' she insisted, desperately trying to hold her position against his clever tactics. 'The house is too small.'

'Then you know the answer. Move back to Elm Ridge, which is big enough for all of us.'

'Never. It's all over. You've got to accept that.'

'And suppose I don't choose to?' His voice was quiet, but the undertone of stubborn determination still throbbed through it.

'Doesn't anyone else get a say? What about how your family feels?'

'I think I'm doing the best thing for my family.'

She stood silent, wishing he would release her. His closeness, the feel of his hands on her arms, was recalling her reaction to his kiss only a few days ago. She'd thought herself safe until the devastating discovery that he could still play on her senses. Ten years ago, on their first date, he'd touched her carefully, as though fearing to break something precious. She could stand anything but that memory. If only he would let her go...

'Faye...' he said in an almost wondering tone.

'Garth, please...'

'Mummy, Mummy, I've done it.'

The shock made them break apart, staring at each other with startled eyes. Cindy erupted into the room.

'I've done it, Mummy. I've put my things into your room, and I've put everything tidy so that you won't have a mess to clear up. Honestly I have.' She grabbed Garth's hand. 'And I've taken one of your bags up to my room.'

'They're too heavy for you, pet.'

'It was just a little one. We could take the others up and I'll help you unpack. Let's do it now. *Please.*'

Faye met Garth's eyes, expecting to see in them a look of triumph. But instead there was something that might almost have been a plea. For a moment, father and daughter were almost comically alike, their faces both registering an urgent need to have their own way. Against her will, Faye's lips twitched.

'What's funny?' he asked quickly.

'Nothing that you'd understand,' she said with a smile.

'*Mummy!*' said Cindy insistently.

'All right. Help your father unpack.'

Cindy let out a yell of delight. '*Hooray, hooray, hooray! Daddy's home today*! Hooray, hooray…' She repeated the couplet over and over, dancing a little jig of happiness, while Garth stared at her. It was the first time Faye could ever remember seeing him nonplussed.

Adrian appeared and came halfway down the stairs.

'Daddy's back, Daddy's back,' Cindy told him unnecessarily.

'Yes, I know—' Adrian looked awkward. 'Is it really true?'

'Just for a while,' Faye said quickly. 'None of us knows what's going to happen, but we'll try to make his visit nice.'

'Daddy,' Cindy called anxiously over the staircase.

'Coming,' Garth called, and went obediently up the stairs.

Faye had warned Garth that he was Cindy's idol but now, for the first time, he understood that this was the literal truth. Her joy at his arrival had confused him. He'd found himself instinctively clinging to the little girl as his only friend in hostile territory. Her adoration touched his heart and her relief that he'd returned for her birthday, as she thought, gave him a rare twinge of guilt.

It charmed him to discover that everything about her

was emphatic. Neither her actions nor her feelings was moderate. Her enthusiasms filled the horizon, and whatever pleased her was the very best in the whole world. He knew how she felt, for he'd been the same as a child, and his adult single-mindedness had played a large part in his success.

Later that evening he sought her out where she was sitting on the steps of the French windows surveying the tiny garden, and sat down beside her. At that moment he had no other motive than to repay her love by being a good father.

'It's about time we planned your birthday present,' he suggested. 'Why don't you give me a list of what you want and I'll arrange everything?'

Cindy regarded her father in a way that Faye could have warned him meant she had a secret agenda. 'Anything?' she asked.

'Anything.'

'Anything at all?'

'Absolutely anything in the whole wide world,' Garth promised incautiously. 'Tell me what it is.'

'A dog.'

He felt almost ludicrously disappointed. A dog was too easy. It gave him no chance to show Faye that she was wrong about him.

'Of course. I'll get in touch with a good breeder tomorrow,' he said, 'and I'll bring you the best puppy there is.' Then he recalled Faye's accusation that he settled everything without reference to others and, with a feeling of conscious virtue, he amended, 'No, you'll want to choose it yourself. You get the puppy and—I mean, we'll go and pick one out together.' He was learning fast.

Cindy nodded vigorously, beaming. A growing understanding of his daughter made Garth add, 'I expect you already know where to go.'

'That's right. Spare Paws.'

'Pardon?'

'Spare Paws. It's a home for abandoned dogs. I pass it every day on my way to school.'

'Darling, what do you want an abandoned dog for? Do you think I can't afford to buy you one?'

Cindy frowned, not understanding his argument. 'Nobody wants them,' she explained. 'They keep hoping and *hoping* that someone will give them a home.'

Just as she didn't understand his language, so he didn't understand hers. 'I can get you a pedigree puppy,' he protested, 'with a good bloodline—'

'But Daddy, people always give homes to pedigree puppies. I want a dog that nobody else wants.'

Garth ran a hand through his hair. 'But you won't know anything about this animal,' he argued. 'It might be full of diseases or fleas—'

'No, Spare Paws always gets its dogs clean and healthy before it lets them go,' Cindy contradicted him gently but firmly.

'Do they also make sure the dogs are friendly? Suppose this creature is vicious? No, darling, it's too chancy. You can choose a puppy from a breeder—'

'I don't *want* to,' Cindy said, sticking her bottom lip out. 'I want a dog that nobody else wants, one who's old and ugly, and blind in one eye, with a leg missing, and—and lots and lots and lots of fleas. And if I can't have that I don't want one at all.' She got up and ran away before Garth could reply.

A choke of laughter from behind made him look up to find Faye regarding him. 'If you'll pardon the pun, you made a real dog's breakfast of that,' she told him.

'Thank you,' he said, chagrined.

'Cindy doesn't care about bloodlines. She wants a dog who needs her love.'

'Isn't that true of any dog?'

'Yes, but it's more true if they're abandoned. And that matters to her.'

'The whole idea is impractical. I'm sorry. She can have a dog, but not like this.'

'We'll see.'

'I'm not going to change my mind.'

Faye took a deep breath. 'Well, it doesn't matter whether you do or not, because you don't make the decisions in this house,' she said calmly.

He scowled but she met his eyes.

'You're trying to make me sound unreasonable when I'm just being sensible,' he argued. 'That's very unfair tactics.'

'Well, if we're going to talk about unfair tactics, what about you barging in here?' she said indignantly.

To her surprise his manner held a touch of sheepishness.

'I used any method that would work,' he admitted.

'Anything that would get your own way,' she said lightly.

He grinned, and for a moment there was a touch of the old, boyish charm. 'It's what I'm good at.'

'Not as good as your daughter. I can't think who she gets it from, but she could give you lessons. Go and do your arguing with Cindy. My money's on her.'

CHAPTER THREE

CINDY was far too generous to exult over her victory but when they set off to Spare Paws, on the day before her birthday, there was a skip in her step.

They were met by Kelly, a pleasant woman in her late thirties, who greeted Cindy as an old friend.

'Cindy often helps us raise funds,' she explained. 'We're a charity, and we only exist through people's kindness.'

'Then perhaps this will help,' Garth said, scribbling a cheque.

Kelly's eyes widened at the sum. 'That's very generous, Mr Clayton.'

Cindy squeezed her father's hand gratefully. 'Can we buy some dog biscuits?' she begged, indicating a table where small bags of biscuits were on sale for a nominal price.

'It's hard to stop people feeding the dogs,' Kelly explained, 'so we provide these. Then we know what they're getting.'

Garth stocked up on biscuits. A very young kennel maid called Jane came to fetch Kelly to the phone, and take over her job of conducting the visitors.

'It's my first week here,' she confided to the children. 'I love them all so much that I'd like to take every one home with me.'

The place was overflowing with dogs, in cages that stretched in all directions. Smiling kennel maids passed down the lines with bowls of food. A tall woman in jeans and sweater appeared with six leads in her hand, calling, 'Who's next for walkies?'

'Some of them are never going to leave us,' Jane said with a sigh. 'They're too old, or there's something wrong with them. So we try to make this a home for them.'

The atmosphere was cheerful. Every dog was an individual to be called by name with a friendly pat and a smile. But they were unwanted by the world. Most still had the desperate eagerness of those who clung to hope, and they barked and bounced to attract attention. Others sat in the resigned silence of creatures who'd been passed over too often.

'I want them all,' Cindy said plaintively.

'I know,' Faye sighed. 'It's heartbreaking, isn't it? But we can only have one, darling.'

Jane took several dogs out of their cages to be properly introduced. Cindy hugged them, but none seemed to be exactly what she was looking for.

'I'll know when I find it,' she said in answer to Garth's query.

'How?' he persisted.

'I'll just *know*.'

'I remember hearing you say that in exactly the same tone,' Faye reminded him. 'You'd just got your first builder's yard and you were choosing a foreman. You picked the strangest looking man because you just *knew* he was ideal.'

'And I was right, wasn't I?'

'Oh yes,' she said with a smile. 'Your instinct was always right.' She spoke amiably because the sun and the pleasant atmosphere were affecting her mood. Garth was behaving well, holding Cindy's hand and attending to her. Whatever his motives, Cindy was so happy at this moment that Faye would have forgiven him much.

He'd done something else, too, that had put him in her good books. Seeing her come downstairs in her buttercup-yellow shirt and fawn trousers he'd observed, 'You've lost weight. About twenty pounds I'd say.'

'Only fourteen,' she said regretfully. 'But I'm fighting for another seven.'

'Go for it! You look terrific.'

Since she'd struggled and fought for her weight loss, she appreciated this more than she would have admitted. Kendall's reaction, 'But you were fine as you were', though kindly meant, had been lacking something. Now she knew what it was.

'Oh, Daddy, look!' the little girl said suddenly. 'Poor doggy! He's so sad.'

The biggest St Bernard Faye had ever seen was regarding them soulfully. His great jowls hung from his face, and his eyes were those of one who carried weighty burdens with dignity. When Cindy called to him, he came eagerly to the wire of his cage.

'I want to hug him,' she told Jane earnestly.

'Is that wise?' Faye asked as Jane unlocked the cage. 'He's ten times her size.'

'Don't worry, he's the gentlest dog we've got,' Jane assured her.

'St Bernards are always gentle,' Adrian said. 'They're docile and obedient, and very intelligent. That's why they're used for mountain rescue.'

'Where did you get that?' Garth asked, for it was clear the boy was quoting.

'From Ken,' Adrian said. 'He knows a lot about them.'

Garth's face clouded but he said no more. Cindy was

hugging the huge dog, who received her caresses eagerly. Benevolence beamed from his eyes, and he uttered a bark of approval that almost deafened everyone.

'His name's Barker,' Jane said, uncovering her ears, 'because that's what he is.'

As if in confirmation Barker promptly boomed again.

'His owner died six months ago,' Jane told them. 'He didn't have any family, and it's hard to find him a new home, because he's so big.'

'He's lovely,' Cindy enthused, burying her face in the thick, brown and white fur.

'Yes, he is,' Adrian said, stroking the huge head gently.

'Hey, kids, come on,' Faye said in alarm. 'He's too big for us, as well. We can't have him in our little house.'

'Why not?' Garth demanded. 'There are fields at the back where you can take him for exercise. He looks a terrific dog to me.'

Barker offered a paw, which both the children solemnly shook.

'Daddy, he wants to shake hands with you,' Cindy said.

Under Faye's incredulous eye, Garth took the huge powder puff offered to him. 'Pleased to meet you, sir,' he declared.

This was obviously the right response for both children, who beamed. Garth ran his hands over Barker's vast frame and offered him a biscuit, which vanished with the speed of light. Another went the same way. The next moment Barker's head was resting in Garth's hands, his eyes suggesting that this was his first food for a month.

'He likes you, Daddy,' Cindy said, delighted.

'Yes, I think he does. Hey, you're a splendid fellow, aren't you?'

Barker agreed, his eyes fixed on the biscuits.

Faye was growing more nervous. 'Don't encourage them,' she told Garth. 'It's out of the question.'

'Why is it, if they want him?'

'In that little house?'

He glanced up and her suspicions were confirmed. 'I know what you're up to and it won't work,' she told him in an undervoice. 'Garth, I'm not going to be manipulated like this.'

He moved aside with her, out of the children's hearing. 'Why must you always think the worst of me?'

'Eight years of marriage.'

'Ten,' he said at once.

'Only eight that counted.'

His eyes gleamed sharply, but he didn't retort.

'I know what you're doing,' she persisted, 'and you've got to stop.'

But Cindy was pulling on her hand, pleading, 'Mummy, Daddy, I want Barker.'

'Darling, he's far too big,' Faye said urgently.

'No, he isn't, he's just right,' Cindy said. 'I love him, and he loves me, and he *wants* to come with us.'

'Of course he does,' Garth said, refusing to meet his wife's eyes. 'You can't disappoint him now.'

She was speechless at his sheer lack of scruple. Under the guise of being kind to his daughter, Garth was arranging matters his own way, as always.

But when they reached Kelly's office it seemed he was due for a setback. While the children played outside with their new friend, Kelly said, 'You shouldn't really have met Barker, but Jane's still new here. He's a permanent resident.'

'But why?' Garth demanded. 'He looks fine to me.'

'He's a lovely dog, but also a very old one. Generally the larger the dog, the shorter the life. Barker's ten, and many St Bernards die at ten. It would be better to choose a younger animal. It's not too late.'

But it *was* too late, as the children's glowing faces confirmed. Through the window they could be seen climbing over Barker, who cheerfully accepted their attentions. Faye made a last attempt to change their minds, but their response was to tighten their arms around their new friend and look mulish.

Kelly made a start on the paperwork. 'He doesn't actually become yours for another month,' she said. 'First I must visit you and see how he is. If your home doesn't seem suitable, then I'm afraid I have to take him back.'

'Don't worry. He'll have the best of everything,' Garth assured her.

While Kelly left them a moment, Faye said angrily, 'That's the worst thing I've ever seen you do. He isn't going to live long. But you don't care if they're hurt so long as you get your way.'

'Faye, Cindy's *happy*.'

'Because she thinks this means her father loves her.'

'Are you saying I don't love my children?'

'Maybe you love Adrian, because he's your son. But Cindy's always been an afterthought to you. How is she going to feel when Barker dies?'

'I'll get her another dog.'

'Another one won't be the same.'

'I'll get one who looks just like him.'

She looked at him in pity. 'You don't understand a thing, do you?'

Kelly returned before he had to answer. The formalities were completed, and they were free to take Barker home.

Garth's big car suddenly looked much smaller when it had to accommodate a hundred and twenty pounds of dog. He took up most of the back seat, with Cindy and Adrian squeezing into whatever was left. When he woofed, Garth and Faye had to rub their ears.

It was Cindy's birthday next day. Faye's gift was a dressing-table set, and a new pair of jeans suitable for a little girl who enjoyed muddy pursuits. Adrian had bought her a video of her favourite television programme. And because Faye had done some inspired last-minute shopping, there was even a new T-shirt bearing a picture of a St Bernard, and a tag that said, 'To Cindy, with love from Barker.'

Garth's present was Barker himself, but Faye knew he wouldn't feel he'd done the job properly unless he'd spent money. She'd wondered wryly how he would rise to the challenge of buying something for a little girl he knew nothing about, but she'd underestimated him. He had an excellent, motherly secretary, who spent the lunch hour shopping and returned with a small coral necklace and matching bracelet. They were exquisite, and Cindy was thrilled.

When she'd opened her cards and presents, she willingly turned the spotlight onto Adrian.

'He's got a very important football match this afternoon,' she explained to Barker. 'And we're going along to cheer. I'll tell you all about it when we come back.'

Promptly at eleven o'clock Adrian was collected by the father of a team-mate, ferrying five players to the match site ten miles away. The rest of the family would follow an hour later.

Cindy was ready well before time, bouncing up and

down with excitement. 'Come *on*, Daddy,' she pleaded. But when he appeared, her expression changed to one of horror. 'Daddy, you *can't* go like that.'

'What's wrong with it?' Garth asked, looking down at his neat, conservative suit.

'Nobody dresses like that,' Cindy said urgently.

'I do.'

'Nobody does.'

'Faye, do you know what this child is talking about?'

'You're overdressed,' she said. 'You should be in jeans and sweater like the rest of us.'

'Does it really matter?'

'Garth, if you turn up dressed for a board meeting, your children will be so embarrassed that they'll pretend not to know you.'

Garth was about to say that his faithful little defender would never deny him, when he caught a look on Cindy's face, and thought better of it. 'I don't have any jeans,' said the man who'd once lived in them, morning, noon and night.

'Something casual, then.'

Between them Faye and Cindy went through his clothes and found garments that Cindy said, 'wouldn't be too cringe-making'. Much chastened, Garth donned trousers and a casual shirt, and they were ready to leave.

'Goodbye, Barker,' Cindy said, hugging him fiercely. 'Be good while we're gone.'

But it seemed that the faithful hound had no intention of staying behind. He followed her to the door, slipped out and went to sit beside the car. When Garth seized his collar and tried to command him back inside, Barker took root in the ground and looked hurt.

'He's afraid to be on his own,' Cindy explained, 'in case we don't come back.'

'He's a dog, not a person,' Garth protested.

But it seemed that Cindy was right. Having lost one owner, Barker was determined not to lose another. As soon as the car door was opened he dashed inside. Cindy followed him and they sat together, determination written on both faces.

'You might as well give in now,' Faye said, stifling a laugh.

'Do you know what that dog's doing to my upholstery? I've just had it cleaned from bringing him home yesterday.'

'I think it's going to need cleaning again,' she observed with apparent sympathy. 'The trouble is that he's so big. But, as I recall, you wanted a big dog.'

'You're enjoying this, aren't you?'

'Who, me?' she asked innocently. In fact, there was a certain satisfaction in the sight of Garth hoist with his own petard.

He started the car, but immediately flinched away, rubbing his ear. 'Cindy, if you don't stop that animal licking me I'll leave you both behind.'

'Barker,' Cindy reproved him, 'you're a very naughty boy.'

Barker barked. Garth winced. Faye dissolved in laughter.

At the match site there was more of an audience than Garth had expected for a schoolboys' game.

'It's the inter-schools trophy,' Cindy explained to him. 'This is the quarter finals, and this year we've got a real chance of winning. Adrian's terribly good. Ken says so.'

'Ken?'

'He's Mummy's friend,' Cindy said innocently, 'and he coaches the football team.'

'He probably won't be here today,' Faye said quickly.

'He's not really the coach, he just fills in sometimes for the fun of it because the real coach has been poorly. But he's well now, so I doubt if Ken—oh, dear.'

Garth followed her eyes to where Adrian's team had appeared, accompanied by a large, bearded man.

'That, I take it, is Kendall Haines?'

'Yes, but I truly thought he wouldn't be here. He was rushing to finish a book before the deadline.'

Garth hardly heard her. He was watching his son claim Kendall's attention with a question that seemed urgent. Kendall answered at length, with gestures towards the field, while Adrian nodded and seemed happier for what he'd heard. He was completely absorbed, and only when the teams ran onto the pitch did he look at the sidelines for his family.

Faye and Cindy led the cheering from the start, yelling loudest whenever their team did well. When Adrian scored in the first half-hour they crowed with delight. So did Barker. Garth tried to catch his son's eye and finally managed it, giving him a thumb's-up sign that Adrian acknowledged with a grin. But it was Kendall's cry of 'Well done, Adrian,' that really delighted him.

Garth thought of where he ought to be right now, the meetings he'd had to cancel, the lame excuses he'd made. And for what? To be forced to watch a demonstration of his son's allegiance to another man.

Then he felt Cindy's tight grip on his hand and looked down at her with a smile. She was his protector, he thought, astonished. Faye was reserved, except when she was laughing at him, and Adrian still maintained a slight distance. It was Cindy who secured his place in the family.

He felt a rare pang of guilt. He was working skilfully to stay in his daughter's good books, because he needed her. And that meant Faye was right, he realized. He was giving Cindy a raw deal. And not for the first time. Her eyes, shining up at him, were uncritical and full of trust and for an instant he had to look away. How could any man meet that honest gaze without a touch of shame?

'Is anything wrong, Daddy?' she asked.

'No. I was just thinking how pretty you are.'

She beamed and clasped her second hand over his with a sigh of contentment. After a moment he bent down and kissed the top of her head.

In the end, Adrian's goal was the only one and his victorious team carried him from the field. His family walked over to where he was being pummelled joyfully.

'Well done, son,' Garth told him.

Adrian turned shining eyes on him. 'Did you really see my goal?' he asked.

'Every moment of it.'

'I thought you weren't going to be here,' Faye said quietly to Kendall. 'You said you had a book to finish.'

'I got it done last night.' He glanced at Garth. 'Is that—?'

'Yes, that's Garth.'

Kendall made a wry face. 'I wish he wasn't quite so good-looking.'

'Don't say things like that,' she urged. 'He means nothing to me now.'

Garth turned his head at that moment and she wondered how much he'd heard. She made the introductions, and to her relief her husband reacted civilly. So did Kendall but she could see the two men sizing each other up, and the knowledge was there between them.

Garth congratulated Kendall politely on his team's success, but this proved unfortunate as it gave Adrian the chance to say, 'Ken's the best coach we've ever had. He knows everything about soccer.'

'Nonsense, you did it all yourself,' Kendall said, aiming a playful punch at him. 'Golden feet, that's what you've got.'

'Am I really going to be good enough to play professionally?' Adrian asked, his face shining.

The sight hurt Garth and prompted his demon to say, 'It's a bit soon to be asking that, isn't it? After all, this isn't the only thing in life.'

He regretted the words instantly, because a light went out of Adrian's face. But he brightened again when Kendall said, 'Keep up the hard work, and you can do anything you want.'

Barker, evidently feeling that he'd taken a back seat long enough, gave his noisiest woof.

'Barker thinks so too,' Cindy confirmed.

'Is he yours?' Kendall asked.

'Daddy gave him to me for my birthday.'

'He's a fine fellow.' Kendall ran his hands knowledgeably over Barker's frame and tried to look into his mouth, but Barker wriggled free in order to sniff one of Kendall's pockets. 'All right,' Kendall said hastily. 'Don't tear me to pieces. I know what you're after. Here!' He produced something which he tossed to the dog, who swallowed it in one gulp.

'What was that?' Faye asked.

'Aniseed. Dogs love it, and I always keep some aniseed sweets in my pocket for my own dogs.'

'Just for the dogs?' Adrian asked cheekily.

'Meaning that I swipe some for myself?' Kendall asked, all innocence. 'Me?'

'Of course not,' Cindy assured him with a carefully

bland face. 'We know you wouldn't *ever* eat aniseed when there was a starving dog who just loved it.'

Kendall grinned and tossed the 'starving dog' another sweet. 'Shame on you, you terrible brats!'

Both children giggled, evidently finding this form of address acceptable. Garth's hands balled into fists inside his pockets.

'Is Barker all right?' Cindy asked.

'He's fine, but don't let him eat too many sweets,' Kendall said, straight-faced. 'He mustn't put on weight.'

'The voice of the expert,' Garth said in a tone that was apparently friendly, but had a slight edge.

'I don't call myself an expert,' Kendall said. 'Not next to my friend, James Wakeham. He's made a special study of St Bernards and he's one of the finest veterinary surgeons in the world. We were at vet school together; used to pinch each other's girlfriends. He was always in trouble. In fact, he owes me a favour for keeping quiet about— Well, never mind. He could have been thrown out for it.' He was talking for the sake of talking, saying anything to lighten the atmosphere. Garth responded with a mechanical smile.

While Cindy asked more questions about Barker's care, Garth found something else to look at.

'This is Ken's subject,' Faye urged him in an under-voice. 'If he needed advice about business, he'd have to come to you.'

'But he never would need advice about business, would he?' Garth growled. 'I know his kind. He floats loftily above money as though the rest of us were beneath contempt. For pity's sake, I gave her the damned dog!'

'Then why don't *you* tell her how to look after him?'

'What time have I got to study dogs?'

'You're the man who believes in keeping track of your investments,' she reminded him. 'And this sudden rush of concern for Cindy is just that—an investment.'

'You're determined to think the worst of me, aren't you?'

'You make it easy,' she said after a moment, and turned away from him.

They were both relieved when the awkward meeting was over. Adrian parted reluctantly from Kendall, promising fervently to be at the next practice.

'As long as you don't neglect your schoolwork,' Garth said. 'You've got a career to think of.'

Adrian became absorbed in Barker, and didn't reply. It was Kendall who said quietly, 'Surely he's a bit young to be deciding his career! If he wants to be a sportsman why not let him dream his dreams and believe he can do anything?'

'Because the world is a tough place, and a man has no time for dreams in case he falls behind,' Garth snapped. 'And I'll thank you not to interfere in my son's upbringing.'

'Hey, come on! I was only—'

'I know damned well what you were *only* doing. And you'll do it over my dead body.'

Luckily Faye had gone ahead and didn't hear this exchange. Garth was able to conceal his unsettled state of mind on the journey home. They'd meant to go to a restaurant but, since Barker refused to be left behind, this was abandoned in favour of a Chinese takeaway.

Later that night, when Garth had gone in to say good-night to Cindy, she heaved a sigh of delight. 'Oh, Daddy, wasn't Adrian simply *super*?'

'He was pretty good,' Garth agreed.

'He was more than good,' Cindy said fervently. 'He

was the very, *very* best. I wish I could do something as well as that.'

Garth brushed her cheek with a finger. 'Don't put yourself down. There must be things you do well.'

'Not as good as Adrian. I'm going to clean the boots he played in this afternoon,' she added in tones of ecstasy. 'He says I can.'

Neither his best friends nor his worst enemies would have called Garth a New Man, but this moved him to protest. 'Let him clean his own boots. You're not his skivvy.'

'But I want to.'

Garth gave up. His daughter's eyes were shining with hero-worship. He wasn't deeply perceptive where feelings were concerned, but he guessed that the need to idolize was a part of her character.

That was dangerous, he thought. A girl who worshipped blindly was vulnerable to the wrong man. She would have to be protected...

Another pair of adoring eyes came into his mind. That was how Faye had looked at him once. She'd loved keeping house for him, ironing his shirts with the same pride as Cindy showed at cleaning her brother's boots. He remembered how her single-minded, vulnerable adoration had been there on her face for all to see. When had she changed into the stranger who kept her thoughts aloof from him?

'Go to sleep, now,' he said abruptly.

'Goodnight, Daddy. Thank you for the best birthday ever.' Her arms were tight around his neck.

'Was it really the best birthday ever?' he asked with rare humility.

'Oh, yes, because you came back for it.'

'Of course I did,' he said, hoping she couldn't see his

sudden awkwardness. 'I'm still your Daddy. Nothing can ever change that.'

'No,' she said happily. 'Nothing, ever.'

'Goodnight, darling.' He kissed the top of her head and went out, thoughtful.

As soon as he arrived at his office on Monday, he instructed his secretary to get him a book on dog care, with special reference to St Bernards. She provided an impressive-looking volume by lunchtime, and over a quick sandwich he flicked through it.

By the end of the day Garth was feeling hard-pressed and out of sorts. A supplier had let him down on delivery dates, one client had backed out of negotiations at the last minute, and another one was trying to wriggle out of payment on a flimsy excuse.

But none of this had annoyed him half so much as discovering that the dog book contained a chapter by Kendall Haines.

CHAPTER FOUR

GRADUALLY they settled into an uneasy truce. Faye couldn't live at such close quarters and not be aware of Garth. The sheer animal force that had made him supreme in his world was reflected in every move he made. About the house she tried to avoid all physical contact, knowing that it wouldn't be safe.

One evening he asked casually, 'Do anything interesting today?'

'Yes, I went to see Kendall.'

'Was that really necessary?'

'Why shouldn't I visit my fiancé, Garth?'

His lips tightened but he said no more, and Faye didn't offer any further explanation.

In fact, her visit to Kendall hadn't been the comfort she'd hoped. She'd poured out her worries, hoping to find understanding, but Kendall had frowned and said lightly, 'Must you spoil our few moments together by talking about your husband all the time?'

'I'm sorry,' she'd said stiffly. 'I didn't mean to be a bore.'

He'd apologized nicely, but the fact remained Kendall liked her whole attention, and was irked because he no longer had it. Was that what had made him suggest that she move back to Elm Ridge, as Garth wanted?

'It might help get him out of your system again,' he'd pointed out, adding in an undervoice, 'something needs to.'

'That's not fair. It's all over between Garth and me.'

'Well, I certainly hope so, because I'm beginning to find him a very boring third in our relationship. I think a spell in your old home might remind you of what made you leave him.' He grinned. 'Then maybe you'd have eyes for me again.'

'Kendall, I love you. You know I do.'

'Do you?' he asked coolly. 'Or are you just running away from Garth? I want all or nothing from you, Faye. Being your refuge from Garth Clayton just isn't good enough.'

'But you're not. I do love you,' she protested.

'Then we have nothing to fear.'

But she knew there was something to fear, even though, on the surface, she and Garth were managing to get by well enough. She was glad to see that he made an effort to be with Cindy and Adrian. Even so, he often spent Saturday in his office and arrived home with a briefcase full of work. Faye and the children would take Barker for a romp in the fields behind the house and get back to find Garth there, poring over his computer.

She had been briefly afraid that he would try to take over her own computer, but after one glance at it he'd roared with laughter. She understood why when she saw his machine, a sleek, state-of-the-art beauty that made her green with envy.

Kendall's assumption that there was nothing to fear troubled her. Despite their mutual hostility, Garth still affected her dangerously. That might seem an argument for going to Elm Ridge, where there was more room, but she knew such a move would be even less safe. Garth would assume he'd won the battle to get her back, and she would never let him think that.

In the end it was Barker who settled the matter in an unexpected way. His idea of fun was to chase madly through the little house, pursued by Adrian, Cindy and herself. Garth never joined in these games, preferring to enjoy the spectacle from the sidelines.

One Saturday afternoon Barker varied the game by raiding the laundry basket. Seeing him trailing clothes, Faye launched herself onto him in a frantic rugby tackle. The children tumbled after her, and the four of them rolled on the floor. It was at this point that Kelly arrived for her check-up visit.

'When I let you have Barker I hadn't realized just how small this place was,' she said worriedly, over a cup of tea. 'A dog his size needs far more room. Your garden is like a pocket handkerchief.'

'But we do take him for walks in the fields at the back,' Faye said.

'Every day?'

'Well, not for the last week,' Faye amended awkwardly. This wasn't the moment to mention the mayhem Barker had caused by chasing squirrels, all of whom had evaded him easily.

Kelly sighed. 'I did say, when I handed him over, that if I wasn't satisfied with his conditions it might be a case for taking him back.'

Cindy and Adrian set up such an outcry that Kelly winced. 'I know it seems hard,' she said, 'but it really isn't kind to Barker to keep him here.'

'But we love him,' Cindy said desperately. 'And he loves us. You can't take him. Daddy, don't let her take Barker.'

'He can't live in this tiny space,' Kelly repeated.

Garth's eyes, full of a message, met Faye's. She drew a deep breath, knowing how she was being propelled into a decision she'd sworn not to make, yet unable to do anything about it. The children were looking at her frantically as they realized they might actually lose their beloved friend.

'We do have the chance of larger premises, with a huge garden,' Garth said, 'but there are a few problems.'

'There are no problems,' Faye said briskly, realizing that she'd been backed into a corner. 'Elm Ridge is standing empty and we can move in tomorrow. Kelly, why don't you come and see us there next week?'

The children jumped around carolling loudly, while Barker added his voice to the proceedings.

When Kelly had gone, Faye took the tea things into the kitchen. Washing them up would give her thoughts time to calm down. Garth had outmanoeuvred her, but that only increased her determination not to yield any more ground. He came in after a moment.

'I'm glad we got that settled,' he said.

'Garth, don't read too much into this,' Faye warned. 'Nothing has really changed.'

'If you're coming home, I'd say a lot had changed.'

'I'm not "coming home". I'm changing premises, but only for a while. I still want that divorce, and when I've got it I'm going to marry Kendall.'

'Don't you think living with me will make a divorce rather difficult?'

'Can't you understand? I won't be living with you. We'll be under the same roof but not living as man and wife. We'll have separate rooms and live separate lives.'

His expression hardened. 'And what exactly does "separate lives" mean?'

'It means I'm still engaged to Kendall, and I'll see him when I like.'

'And suppose your husband has other ideas?'

'It won't make any difference.'

'So my wishes count for nothing?'

'That's right. You've won a small victory by getting us there, but that's all. I'm not your wife, and I'll do as I please.'

'My God! It's like beating my head against marble,' he said angrily. 'You were never like this before.'

'I've changed, Garth.'

'You sure as hell have!'

'But so have you. You're not the loving man I married, any more than I'm the docile girl you married.' Her lips curved in a faint, elusive smile. 'Watching you taught me a lot about standing on my own feet, and I've learned the lessons well. Just regard me as a housekeeper.'

'I already have one, in Nancy.'

'Well, now you've got two. And, like any housekeeper, I'll live my own life, and my employer won't ask questions.'

'Oh, won't he?'

'Not unless he wants to receive some dusty answers.' Mischievously she echoed his own words, 'I'm glad we got that settled.'

'I haven't—'

'It's settled, Garth. Believe me, it's settled.'

They returned to Elm Ridge to a huge welcome from Nancy, overjoyed, 'to have some life in the place again', as she said to Faye over a coffee in the kitchen.

'He's been like a bear with a sore head since you all left. Not that he was ever exactly sweetness and light.'

'He was, once,' Faye mused, then stopped. She'd promised herself not to start looking back, no matter how much the house affected her.

But he *had* been different: not sweetness and light, but generous and passionately loving to her. So many nights of physical rapture in the perfect union of their bodies. So many days of sadness as their minds and hearts grew further apart.

Adrian and Cindy eagerly took possession of their old rooms, then introduced Barker to the huge garden, which he tore around as madly as a puppy. This resulted in his first meeting with Fred, who came in two afternoons a week to keep the grounds in order. Fred was a grumpy individual who had his own views on dogs who trampled across his freshly weeded flower beds, and he expressed them loudly. But by then Barker was out of earshot.

Faye was touched to see that Garth had had her room redecorated in her favourite autumnal colours. On the dressing table lay a gift box, containing a set of emerald earrings.

'They're a welcome present,' he said from the doorway. He seemed almost nervous. 'I can show my gratitude, can't I?'

'Garth, they're really beautiful, and it was sweet of you to think of it, but — '

'Just try them on.'

'You don't have anything to be grateful for. You know why I'm here. I don't think I can accept these.' She extended her hand, with the box.

'Look,' he said with almost a touch of desperation, 'it's your birthday next week. Call it an early birthday present. The children will notice if I don't give you something.'

'You can give me something small. I can't take these.'

He was pale. 'Just as you wish.'

For a moment her resolution faltered. There was a look on his face that took her by surprise. Years ago he'd gone without lunch for a week to buy her a special gift, which had broken as soon as it was opened. His expression then had been the same as now, the look of a hurt boy. He controlled it so quickly that Faye wasn't sure she'd seen it, but she spoke her next words gently. 'Garth, I did tell you—'

'Yes, you made your position very plain. I just hadn't expected you to be so—so unyielding.'

'Maybe I was too yielding in the past.'

'Well, you're sure making up for it now,' he said, going to the door. 'And don't worry. I'm still sleeping in the room downstairs.'

Barker might be a daft mutt, as Faye often complained, but he had a sense of self-preservation that made him spend the first week wooing Nancy. In a few days she'd progressed from 'Get your muddy paws out of my kitchen,' to 'Poor doggie, don't they ever feed you?'

During that week Faye saw little of Garth. She was left in peace to settle herself into her old home, and after the first day she found she could cope. She was grateful for Garth's reticence. On the odd occasions when he was around, he gave all his attention to the children and maintained a civil distance from herself.

Cindy and Adrian were so happy, especially with the huge garden, that Faye knew a twinge of guilt. Had she been selfish in taking them away from this lovely setting? But then she thought of Kendall's spacious premises and his collection of rescued animals. The children loved his home. They would be just as happy there when the time came.

Two days before her birthday Garth gave her his present early. It was a computer, identical to his own, that would be a boon for her book-keeping work. But Faye's reaction was divided between pleasure at the gleaming monster and a suspicion that Garth was muscling in on her territory.

'It's another takeover bid, isn't it?' she demanded.

'What was that?'

'It's a show of power. You're saying that I can't even manage my trivial little job without your guiding hand.'

'Well, I'll be——!' he exclaimed angrily. 'Your tortuous mind is something I'll never figure out. You bend my ear about your independence, and how I'm holding you back. Well, I'll tell you what's holding you back: that steam-age machine you're using! You need a better one. *I was trying to be nice, for Pete's sake!*'

He stormed out, slamming the door. Shocked, Faye realized that he was genuinely upset. She stood for a moment, undecided, before following him into his study.

'I'm sorry,' she said at once. 'I shouldn't have said what I did.'

'You really have got me down as a villain, haven't you?'

'It was unforgivable of me,' she said contritely.

His mouth twisted. 'I never found anything you did unforgivable. But I will if you refuse it.'

She smiled. 'I'm not going to refuse it. I'm going to ask you to show me how to work it.'

'Now you're talking.'

The children were fascinated by the machine, but scandalized to discover what it was for.

'Daddies don't give mummies computers for their birthdays,' Cindy protested.

'You think I should give her something more personal?' Garth mused. 'I'll bear it in mind.'

The next morning Faye was deep in work when the phone rang in Garth's study. Nancy was out shopping and Faye was alone in the house. She hurried in and snatched the receiver up so quickly that she dropped it. The weight pulled the whole machine off the desk, forcing her to scrabble on the floor. By the time she'd retrieved everything the woman on the other end was already talking.

'Couldn't think where you'd got to.' She gave a husky laugh. She sounded young, and there was a note of intimacy in her voice. 'You're usually so punctual that we could set the clock by you.'

'Excuse me?' Faye said.

After a brief pause the woman said, 'I thought I was talking to Mr Clayton. Evidently not.'

'No, I'm—'

'I've called to find out if anything's happened to him. He's usually at work by now.'

'He left at the usual time this morning,' Faye said. 'Perhaps he got stuck in some traffic. By the way, my name's—'

'He's got a client due in a few minutes,' the young woman cut across her. 'It's not like him to miss an appointment.'

'Then I'm sure he'll be there,' Faye replied in a voice that held an edge of annoyance at the woman's rudeness. 'Are you his secretary?'

'Don't be ridiculous,' the young woman said frostily. 'Of course I'm not a secretary. I am Lysandra Bates, the Director of Publicity for Clayton Properties. I can't waste time talking. If Garth calls, I want you to give him a message from me.'

'I'm afraid I'm not a secretary either,' Faye said, feeling bolshie.

'All right, all right, so you're the housekeeper, cleaning woman, whatever,' Lysandra snapped. 'And I suggest you keep a civil tongue in your head, whoever you are. Write this down, and don't waste any more of my time.'

'Actually, I'm Garth's wife,' Faye said, goaded into one of her rare tempers.

She had the satisfaction of knowing that she'd silenced the other woman. After a moment Lysandra Bates said tensely, 'I had no idea— That is, I understood— *Mr Clayton, I've been worried about you.*' She turned back to the phone. 'He's just arrived. Crisis over.'

'I'm so glad,' Faye said politely.

'Good day to you.'

'And good day to *you*,' Faye murmured, regarding the phone, which had gone dead before she could reply.

Nancy put her head around the door. 'I'm back. Want a coffee?'

'Yes please, and make it strong. I need something after that. Have you come across Lysandra Bates, Nancy?'

'Oh, her,' Nancy said in a voice of deep significance.

'I didn't like her either,' Faye said, following Nancy into the kitchen. 'She thought I was the housekeeper.'

'And she talked as if she had a bad smell under her nose,' Nancy supplied.

'Exactly. She's obviously called before. So how come she didn't realize that I wasn't you? Our voices are quite different.'

'She wouldn't notice that, although goodness knows, she's telephoned often enough. To Miss Bates all underlings are beneath her notice.'

'You say she telephones often?'

'Every time she can find an excuse. Once, she turned up with some papers she *said* Mr Clayton needed. I thought he looked a bit surprised myself. Oh, she'd like to make herself at home here. But of course,' she added hastily, 'it's all on her side.'

'It's all right, Nancy,' Faye said, amused. 'You know this situation isn't permanent.' She'd taken Nancy into her confidence days ago.

'But he wants you back,' Nancy said, scandalized. 'You know he does.'

'Hmm. Just the same, I wouldn't put it past him to have my replacement lined up to massage his ego, just in case. I don't mind if they get together. I just didn't like her being rude to me, that's all.'

'There's nothing in it,' Nancy said firmly. 'Just because she's got an eye for the boss, it doesn't mean that he's got an eye for her.'

'I've told you, I don't care if he is interested in another woman,' Faye said, a tad more sharply than she'd intended.

Nancy gave her an appraising glance, but had the tact to let the subject drop.

When Garth returned that night Faye told him about the call, not mentioning Lysandra's rudeness but only his mysterious lateness for work. To her surprise he reddened, mumbled something and quickly changed the subject.

'I wanted to talk about your birthday,' he said. 'I'd like us to have a family evening out, rather than have you spend it with Haines.'

'That's fine,' she said. 'I was planning to stay with the children anyway.'

He hesitated. 'And you don't mind if I tag along?'

'The kids will never forgive you if you don't.'

The following day he offered Faye a tiny gold watch, delicate, restrained, and impossible to refuse.

'That's why I was late for work yesterday morning,'

he admitted. 'I had to go to three shops to find the right one.' Then, seeing her astonished face, he added hastily, 'But it's just a trifle. Nothing that you can't accept.'

Three shops, she mused. Late for work. *Garth?*

She wore the watch to the restaurant, where the whole family went to celebrate that night. It was a pleasant time, with Garth at his best, talking to Faye in a general way that didn't create any awkwardness, and listening attentively to his children.

'Are you getting excited about Cornwall?' he asked, and both youngsters grinned with delight at the prospect of the school camping trip to come.

But then Cindy said worriedly, 'Will Barker be all right without us?'

'Don't worry, you can leave everything to me,' Garth said easily. He saw Faye's lips twitching and said defensively, 'I can be good at things if I set my mind to it.'

'I know you can,' she admitted.

The meal went slowly, because at every course Cindy insisted on a doggy bag to take some home to Barker.

'What happens if *we* want to eat something?' Garth enquired in a spirit of curiosity. 'This is supposed to be your mother's birthday treat.'

'But Daddy, poor Barker's all alone at home,' Cindy pointed out.

'Well, at least he didn't try to get into the car with us this time,' Garth said with a grin.

'Yes, it was strange how quiet he was,' Faye mused.

'I think this is the best mummy's birthday ever,' Cindy said blissfully. 'And mine was the best *me* birthday ever.'

'What about that time I gave you a bike?' Garth asked. 'You were pretty pleased with that.'

'Oh, yes, it was a lovely bike,' Cindy said politely.

Too late he realized he'd put his foot in it. That had been her last birthday before the split, and he'd spent it the other side of the world. Faye had presented the bike. He sought back for a better birthday memory, and was shocked that he couldn't find one. Surely he couldn't have failed her every time?

'All right,' he said, remembering something with relief. 'How about that birthday when we all went to a burger bar. We had a great time, and I got stomachache from eating burgers and ice cream.'

Cindy crowed with laughter. 'Oh, Daddy, you were so funny that night.'

They'd all made silly jokes and laughed madly. It had been a great night out.

'There you are then. Wasn't that your best birthday?'

But Cindy shook her head. 'That was Adrian's birthday,' she said, not complaining but simply stating the fact.

'Oh, yes,' he said awkwardly, 'so it was.'

He had not seen Faye making frantic signals to him. His heart sank. When had he ever been there for Cindy? He hadn't even bothered to keep her photograph, although he had Adrian's, and Faye's too, hidden away in a drawer where nobody could discover it.

Now he remembered the one time he'd had an attack of conscience, buying her some pretty gift in town, only to discover that it was something she already had, without his even knowing. Faye had told him that. Cindy hadn't mentioned it, only rejoiced over her present like someone offered water in the desert.

Under the table he squeezed her hand, and was rewarded by a look of glowing happiness. For her, the past was forgotten, all swept away by the pleasure of his presence now. What must it be like to be able to forgive so easily?

To cover his confusion he raised his glass and said, 'Happy birthday to Mummy!'

Everyone chorused, 'Happy birthday!' and the moment passed.

The rest of the evening went merrily. When it was time to go, the children solemnly took possession of three doggy bags, treasuring them like gold, and carried them out to the car.

'Not on my freshly cleaned upholstery, *please*,' Garth said faintly.

Nancy had gone to visit her sister. When they drove past the railway station Faye spotted her coming out and they stopped to collect her. As they neared Elm Ridge they were astonished to see two police cars and four men.

'My name's Hallam,' a policeman said as Garth jumped out of the car. 'Your burglar alarm went off in the station. Someone's broken into your house. We're going to investigate.'

Faye and Garth insisted on coming too, leaving the children in Nancy's care. The house was in darkness and looked as always except that the French windows, which opened inward, stood gaping wide.

Quietly they slipped into the dark house and moved up the stairs. A muffled noise came from Cindy's bedroom. 'In there,' Hallam whispered. He took a deep breath and charged into the bedroom. *'OK! Nobody move! You're nicked.'*

The silence that followed had a stunned quality. Following quietly, Garth and Faye were aghast to see Barker stretched out on Cindy's bed, regarding them with sleepy surprise.

Hallam spoke through gritted teeth. *'You left your dog out, sir!'*

Faye crept tactfully away, pausing in the hall to call Nancy on the car phone, and telling her to bring the children in. She made coffee, which slightly mollified the police. But before they departed, Hallam paused in the doorway to say stiffly, 'Perhaps you'd like to consider having your burglar alarm disconnected from the station, sir? *Soon!'*

'Who left that wretched animal out?' Garth demanded when they were alone.

'It was you, Mummy,' Cindy claimed reproachfully. 'You called up the stairs, "Barker's in."'

Faye groaned. 'No, I said, "*Check* that Barker's in." I thought you were going to do it.'

'So nobody did it,' Garth said. 'When he found himself locked out, he simply charged the French windows until they burst open.'

He regarded the miscreant who'd eaten the contents of the doggy bags, and was now making a start on the bags themselves. 'Call yourself a guard dog!' he said accusingly. 'You're supposed to scare intruders away, not open the doors and invite them in.'

'Daddy, are you cross with Barker?' Cindy asked.

'Whatever for?' Garth demanded wildly. 'He's only broken into the house, made a mockery of my alarm system, and turned me into the butt of the local police.' He saw her looking worried and took her into the circle of his arm. 'It's all right, pet. He's forgiven.'

His reward was an eager hug. Even Adrian made a small concession, squeezing his father's shoulder as he went past. Faye followed them upstairs, where Nancy had just finished changing Cindy's bed linen.

'I'm sorry Barker gave you that extra work,' Faye said.

'It's no matter,' Nancy said, casting a benevolent eye on the culprit, who'd trotted up after Cindy. 'The poor dog was lonely.' She scratched Barker's head and he responded with a sigh in which fidelity, forgiveness and noble endurance were perfectly mixed. 'You come with Nancy, darling, and she'll find you a special titbit, to make up for all you've been through.'

CHAPTER FIVE

WHEN Faye had seen the children tucked up she returned downstairs, where Garth was on the sofa drinking brandy. He handed her a glass of sherry that he'd poured for her.

'I thought you might need something to recover,' he said.

'Shall I check that everything's locked up?'

'No, I've just done it. Though it seems a wasted effort,' he observed wryly, 'since we have a dog that's keeping open house. What's so funny?' Faye had given a choke of laughter.

'I'm sorry,' she said. 'I was just trying to recall who said that once we were at Elm Ridge Barker couldn't cause any more trouble.'

Garth grinned. 'He was a short-sighted fool, whoever he was.'

'Oh, dear! That policeman's face!'

He gave a shout of laughter.

'Hush, you'll rouse the house,' she said, but her own mirth was bubbling up. She met his eye and suddenly the joke became hilarious. She leaned back against the sofa and laughed until she nearly cried. To her delight Garth was afflicted the same way. He gripped her hand, and she clasped him back, sharing the moment.

When the attack passed they sat together, giving vent to the occasional chuckle. His glance fell on her hand, still held in his. He grew quite still, then he raised it and brushed it against his cheek.

'What happened?' he asked quietly. 'Once, we were always laughing like that. Where did we lose it?'

At first she couldn't answer. His gesture had taken her breath away.

'It disappeared bit by bit,' she said slowly. 'We grew in different directions.'

'But did we have to? Couldn't we have stopped it?'

'I don't know,' she sighed. 'Perhaps we couldn't. We wanted such different things.'

'I never knew that,' he said after a while. 'I thought we wanted the same.'

'I tried to. When I couldn't see things your way, I pretended I did. But the pretence became too much. Something had to give. I know now that I was never the wife for you.'

'I don't believe that,' he said simply.

He raised her hand again, brushing his lips over the back of it. It was a tender, rather than a lover-like gesture. Garth seemed lost in some private dream, only half-knowing what he did. But Faye was intensely aware of his touch, of the sudden beating of her heart, and of a feeling of danger. For a moment she wanted nothing so much as to throw herself into his arms. But she backed away from the feeling.

'It was a lovely evening, wasn't it?' he said.

'It was wonderful,' she told him sincerely.

He looked down at the hand still clasped in his. It was her left, and a band encircled her wedding finger. 'That's not my ring. Did he give it to you?'

'No. I bought it from a market stall.'

'You don't really belong to either of us, huh?'

'Just myself, for a while. I think I should go to bed now. Thank you for a lovely evening, Garth.'

With an almost inaudible sigh her released her. 'Goodnight, Faye.'

She slipped away hurriedly and didn't stop until she'd closed the door of her bedroom behind her. In a few short moments Garth had approached the very heart that she'd shielded against him. She hadn't meant to let it happen, but his gentle, almost wistful, tenderness had taken her by surprise.

The feelings coursing through her were devastating: an irrational sense of happiness, hope, expectancy. Like a giddy teenager, she thought, when the idol first glanced her way. Like herself, ten years ago. Was that why she had the shocking feeling that she'd betrayed Kendall?

But the children needed their parents to be friendly, she reminded herself. When the divorce finally came, they would be happier, knowing that they didn't have to divide their loyalties.

So that was all right, she thought, with relief. She was only doing what was best for Cindy and Adrian and there was no need to feel guilty.

The end of the school term was in sight. The children had started marking off the days and chanting, 'Twelve more days to the holidays. Eleven more days to the holidays. Ten more days...'

'Mummy, have you signed our forms?' Adrian asked one morning as they were leaving the breakfast table. Garth had already departed.

'Forms?' Faye asked blankly.

'The forms about the end of term party,' Adrian explained. 'You're supposed to sign them to say it's all right for us to be home late that day. We have to take them back this morning.'

'Oh, yes, let me find them.'

'I've just put them in front of you,' Adrian said patiently.

'Sorry. Yes. Fine.' Faye hastily signed, aware that her children were giving her puzzled looks.

'Are you all right, Mummy?' Adrian asked.

'Of course I am, darling.'

'It's just that you've been funny lately,' Cindy said. 'You keep going all vague.'

'Nonsense,' Faye said, shaken by her daughter's perception.

'You do, Mummy,' Adrian insisted. 'We say things, and you don't answer.'

'I've got a lot on my mind. Now come on, you kids. I'm going out to warm the engine. You have ten seconds to explain to Barker that you aren't abandoning him for ever. And Cindy, please try to get it through to him this time, because I don't want any more scratch marks on my car.'

She escaped with relief, but she couldn't relax until she'd delivered them to school and could be alone. It was true that she'd been in a strange mood recently. Since the night of her birthday her mind had been troubled, and so had her heart.

Garth had argued and fought her for weeks and she'd held him off. But that night he'd spoken to her quietly and with a touch of wistfulness. For a few minutes she could almost have believed that the man she'd loved still lived somewhere deep in his shell. When he'd brushed her hand against his cheek in unconscious echo of their first date, her confusion had been so great she'd almost snatched her hand away.

She was in more danger now than she'd been since she confronted him two months ago. Suddenly her heart was dreaming impossible dreams, the kind she'd thought she'd put away for ever. Her head was protesting, telling her to see reason, but the voice of common sense was alarmingly faint.

She ought to visit Kendall and let him reassure her. But suddenly she felt unable to look Kendall in the face.

When she reached home she went, as if by instinct, into the room where she and Garth had sat together that night. There was the sofa on which he'd taken her hand...

Her eyes fell on a folder of papers. She'd seen Garth bring it out of his study that very morning, ready to take to work. And he'd left it behind.

Faye snatched up the phone and dialled his office. She was put through to Mary, Garth's secretary, a pleasant, middle-aged woman whom Faye had met several times and liked.

'Mr Clayton is in a meeting and said he wasn't to be disturbed,' she said. 'Can I help?'

Faye was about to tell her about the papers when she was stopped by the memory of a similar incident, years ago. Garth had been annoyed that she'd innocently revealed to one of his staff that he'd made a mistake. It was part of his creed never to show weakness to employees.

'I really do need to speak to him,' she persisted. 'It's very important.'

'Just one moment.'

Mary's voice became fainter, as though she'd turned away. 'It's Mrs Clayton. What shall I do? He said no interruptions.'

From far back in the room Faye could hear another voice that she recognized as Lysandra Bates. 'Go carefully. She's got to be kept sweet. The anniversary range is really important to Garth. I'd better talk to her myself.'

There was a scuffling sound as the phone changed hands, then the woman spoke again in a tone of professional amiability.

'Good afternoon, Mrs Clayton. I'm Lysandra Bates.'

'Yes, we've talked before,' Faye said pleasantly.

'Oh, that hardly counts, does it?' Lysandra said with a small laugh. 'I've been looking forward to meeting you properly, so that we can talk about the arrangements.'

'Arrangements?' Faye asked.

'The publicity arrangements for the anniversary range. It's so delightful that your tenth wedding anniversary coincides with our new range of family houses. I expect Garth has told you that they're going to be marketed with an emphasis on the stability of family life, and a couple who've been married for ten years just epitomizes stability, don't you think?'

Nobody could have guessed from her tone that only recently she'd been shocked to discover that Faye had returned to her husband's home.

'I'm not quite sure,' Faye said very slowly. She was controlling her words, because the thought that was forming in her head was surely too monstrous to be true.

'Well, I expect you find it hard to visualize,' Lysandra Bates conceded in her sweet, icy voice. 'It'll be easier for you when you see everything laid out. The gist of it is that these are houses where couples will want to raise their families, and no one knows that better than the man who built them, and who's celebrating his own tenth wedding anniversary. And, of course, the children. I am right about that, aren't I? You have two adorable children.'

'I do have two children, but I don't want them made a part of any publicity campaign.'

'Well, we can discuss that later,' Lysandra said dismissively. 'I thought you and I might have lunch one day, to discuss how your anniversary should be presented. My diary's a bit full, but what would you say to the week after next?'

'I'm afraid not.'

'Well, I suppose it's a little far ahead. Perhaps I could squeeze you in—'

'Please don't trouble yourself,' Faye said firmly. 'I'm sure you're much too busy. Good day.'

She hung up and sat there, stunned, thinking how easily she'd been taken in! What a blind fool, to imagine that Garth had changed! She'd known what he was like, yet still she'd let him delude her with a few clever words and a show of attention to Cindy and Adrian.

But underneath he was as bad as ever. No, worse! To exploit his neglected children and his mockery of a marriage, showing the world a false picture of harmony, so that he could make money; even she had never thought he could do anything so monstrous. She could have wept to think of the feelings that had lit up the world for her recently. And it had all been a wicked mockery.

Garth was late home that night and Faye waited until he'd said goodnight to the children before she spoke to him.

'You're very quiet,' he observed.

'That's because I've been doing a lot of thinking.'

'About us?'

'About you. There is no ''us'', and there never will be.'

Something in her voice made him look at her sharply. 'What's up?'

'I've discovered the nasty little game you're playing.'

'Faye, what are you talking about? What "game"? I'm not playing games.'

'Oh, no, the making of money is deadly serious to you, isn't it? How stupid of me to forget it!'

'What's happened?' he asked quietly.

'I called you at work today. You left your papers behind on the sofa. But you were in a meeting and couldn't be disturbed.'

He made a sound of annoyance. 'I'm sorry about that. They should have put you through. Next time—'

'Garth, it's not about that. It's about the anniversary range—or should I say, the *tenth* anniversary range?'

He drew in a sharp breath. 'Damn!'

'Miss Bates naturally assumed I knew, since I'm part of the publicity. I'd have to be, wouldn't I, since you're featuring your happy, united family?'

'Faye, will you just hear me out? I was going to tell you at the proper time, in the proper way.'

'And what would have been the proper time and way to tell your wife that you've been going through the motions of wanting her back so that you could exploit her, and your children? It's all been a wicked pretence; the charming husband, the attentive father—anything to get us back under this roof in time for the press campaign. No wonder you pulled every trick! How could you have sold yourself as the perfect family man while we were living apart?'

'Will you let me speak? It's not the way you think—'

'Garth, you don't know what I think because if you did, you'd shrivel up inside.'

'That's why I didn't tell you before. I knew you'd misunderstand. This isn't a deep laid plot. Actually, it was you who put the idea into my head.'

'Oh, please—'

'It's true. When you came here that first night, everything you said about the tenth anniversary—I'd been searching for an angle for this range and suddenly it all fell into place.'

'And of course you had to make use of it.'

'Yes, I did. You know what I'm like. If a good idea comes to me I'll go for it. You solved a problem I'd been racking my brains over. It was almost like Providence, as though you'd been sent.'

'If that's how you think, I don't wonder you see me only as an adjunct to your business. I came here to talk about the end of a relationship that once meant something to both of us, and you thought Providence had sent me to solve your marketing problems. What were you doing when you kissed me? Conducting a feasibility test?'

'How dare you say that?' he snapped. 'That kiss was real. You knew that at the time; we both did.'

'Nonsense! You were faking. *And so was I.*'

Garth grew very pale and there was a look in his eyes that she'd never seen before. 'Would you like to prove that, right now?'

'Not now or ever. I'll never kiss you again, Garth. It's over. Finished. If there was any hope we could get back together, this kills it. I'm going to have that divorce, any way I can.'

'All right,' he said unexpectedly. 'I'll give you one.'

'What?'

'I'm offering you a deal. Stay here just a few weeks longer. Help me out with this publicity. Play my "game" if you're so sure that's what it is. Then you can have a divorce on any terms you like.'

'I don't believe you,' Faye said slowly. 'This is another trick.'

'I swear it isn't. An easy divorce. Your terms. The only condition I make is that afterwards I see my kids as often as I want—as often as *they* want. And I'll want to see them plenty.'

'You'd better. If you let them down I'll never forgive you.'

'I won't let them down, Faye. Things have changed. You think it's all been an act, but it hasn't. I've learned to appreciate them now and I'm grateful to you for helping me do that. But I need your help again, one last time. Cooperate over the tenth anniversary, and I'll never ask you for anything else again.'

'What exactly do you want me to do?'

'Stay here. Let the world think we're a happy family. And don't see Kendall Haines.'

Faye gave a bitter laugh to cover the pain. 'I see. This is nothing but an excuse to stop me seeing my fiancé.'

'Don't call him that,' Garth snapped.

'It's what he is. Oh, Garth, you're so transparent! You really thought I'd be daft enough to fall for this one? Kendall is the man I'm going to marry and you're not going to separate me from him. And if that spoils your publicity, why don't you hire someone from Central Casting? She'd probably make a better job of pretending to be your wife than I would.'

'You don't give an inch, do you?' Garth said bitterly.

'I feel safer that way.'

She left the room before he could answer and slipped away into the grounds, where she could lose herself among the bushes. At last she sat down on a tree stump and stared out at the stars. It was all so beautiful and peaceful, but there was no peace in her heart.

She covered her eyes, trying to fight back the tears.

She knew that only strength would help her now, but she didn't seem to have any left.

She felt a freezing shock against her fingers, as though an ice cube had touched them. It turned out to be Barker's nose. He'd followed her.

'It's all right,' she said, drying her eyes. 'Everything's fine.'

He pushed his head under her hand and looked at her out of beautiful eyes. He didn't believe her.

'You're a lovely old boy, aren't you?' Faye said, putting her arms around him. It was a relief to hug the sturdy body and hide her face in his thick coat. Barker's tail thumped the ground. He was doing what he did best.

As a child, Faye had confided her small tragedies to an all-wise teddy bear. Now there was Barker, warm and responsive, who would listen without judgement and break no confidences.

'I've been so stupid,' she told him sadly. 'I thought I was strong enough to cope with Garth, but I was kidding myself. I wanted him to be like he was before: wonderful. And that was really silly of me, wasn't it?'

His eyes were so full of understanding that it was almost as if he'd spoken. *Anyone had the right to be silly.*

'Yes, but I was worse than silly, because I know what he's like, yet I still let myself— Well, anyway it's over between us.'

A small crease appeared between Barker's eyes. *Sure about that?*

'It was over two years ago,' she said, fondling his soft ears. 'I love Kendall now.'

At the sound of Kendall's name, Barker gave the soft, yearning woof of a dog who'd discovered aniseed and never forgotten his benefactor.

'You're perfectly right,' Faye said, brightening. 'Kendall's the one I need to talk to.' She rubbed Barker's head gratefully. 'Why didn't I think of that myself?'

He sighed. *Because you're not crazy about aniseed.*

She knew Garth was watching as she drove away. He would guess, of course, where she was going but she was too angry to care.

Kendall received her news thoughtfully. 'And this way we'd be sure of getting the divorce?' he asked.

'So he says. How do I know he'd stick to that?'

'Oddly enough, I believe he would. I don't like your husband, but I think he's a man of his word.'

'You're right,' Faye said slowly. 'But still—it would mean we wouldn't be able to see each other for weeks.'

'We might sneak the occasional meeting.'

'No,' she said regretfully. 'I can't expect Garth to keep his word if I don't keep mine. We must stay apart, to make sure we can be together afterwards.'

'As long as it doesn't go on too long,' he said. 'You know this is a risk. If you don't love me as much as you say—'

'But I do,' she said firmly. 'You know that.'

'Yes, of course I do.'

Barker greeted her as soon as she returned home, eagerly sniffing her hands and pockets. When he found no aniseed he gave her the indignant look of a dog who'd been thoroughly conned. Faye pushed him aside with difficulty and went to Garth's study, firmly shutting the door.

Despite the late hour he was still up, working. He pushed the work away and regarded her tensely. He looked tired and he'd torn open the front of his shirt, as though he needed to breathe more easily.

'I've been to see Ken,' she told him. 'We've talked it over and he thinks I should do this. So you've got your deal.'

Instead of pleasing Garth, this seemed to annoy him. 'I don't need that man's permission for anything I want to do,' he growled.

'Not his permission, his blessing,' she retorted. 'I wouldn't do it without that. You said yourself I don't belong to either of you. But if I did it would be Ken, not you.'

'You'll never belong to any other man,' Garth said with a sudden flash of temper. 'As long as I want you, *you belong to me*.'

'As long as you want me,' Faye echoed. 'But you didn't want me very long, did you, Garth? Not really want *me*. A mother to your children, yes. But when I grew up you were either hostile or indifferent. A divorce will be as good for you as for me. Then you can marry a doll who'll never answer back.'

'You know nothing about me if you can say a damned fool thing like that.'

'Well, perhaps I never did really know you,' she agreed. 'Or you me. It's better this way. I'll stay with you until the marketing campaign is launched, but only to get the divorce. And I have conditions too.'

'Which are?'

'We leave the children out of it. They're not going to be involved in the publicity. And I won't stop them seeing Ken.'

'I'd rather they didn't.'

'I'm sorry, those are my terms. They like him. Cindy calls him for advice about Barker and Adrian is involved with one of Ken's countryside campaigns. I don't want you worrying them with our private quarrels.'

'And the other condition?' he asked.

'You stay right away from me, or the deal's off.'

'I suppose Haines thought of that one?'

'No, it's all my own idea. I want your solemn promise.'

He sighed. 'Very well. You have my word.'

'So that's settled.' She waited, wondering if he would say something more, but he only shrugged. Once Garth had concluded a deal on the best terms he could get, it wasn't his way to waste time on a post-mortem.

'I hope this means that we won't argue so much, Garth.'

'I've never liked arguing with you.'

'No, you just prefer me to give in without a fight,' she said lightly. 'But this is a business arrangement. Nothing more.'

'Nothing more,' he murmured.

'I'll keep my side and I expect you to keep yours.'

Garth leaned back and regarded her with a wry grin. 'You've become a tough negotiator. You know what you want, and you won't settle for less.'

'You should offer me a job with your firm. I seem to have all the qualifications.'

'Well, maybe I— What the devil is the matter with that dog? He's been trying to scratch the door down ever since you came in here.'

'I'll see to him, then I'm going to bed.'

'Won't you join me in a drink, to celebrate our deal?'

She hesitated. 'No, but I'll shake hands with you, if you will.'

He looked at her little hand, firmly outstretched to him. After a while he took it gently in his own. 'To business,' he said.

'To business. Goodnight, Garth.' She left the room

without looking back, so she didn't see him staring after her.

She had a curious sensation of light-headedness. It felt good to have made a stand, and actually stopped the Garth Clayton juggernaut in its tracks.

She wasn't left to muse for long. Barker, bent on sorting out the misunderstanding, followed her upstairs and waited determinedly in the hall while she kissed her sleeping children.

When she emerged he planted himself firmly in her path. But this, too, failed. Faye hugged him and called him loving names, but there was no aniseed. At last he accepted the perfidy of humans, and retired to his basket in a huff.

CHAPTER SIX

IT WAS halfway through Saturday morning when Garth received a phone call from Bill, his second in command and the one person who knew all his business secrets.

'Garth, sorry to call you at home on a Saturday.'

'That's all right. You know I'm never really off duty.'

'I tried the office first. It felt strange not to find you there.'

'Yes, I've been spending a little more time at home recently,' Garth said, hoping his edginess couldn't be heard in his voice. He'd made a special effort to be at home today, meaning to spend some time with his son, only to find that Adrian had other plans. Even Cindy wasn't there to support him, having taken Barker to spend the day with Jenny Patterson, her best friend.

An hour later Kendall had collected the boy in his old van. Garth had longed for Adrian to tell him where they were going and why, but when he didn't Garth shrugged and refused to show how much he minded.

'What's it all about?' he asked now.

'It's the Outland,' Bill said, naming a patch of land about twenty miles away on which Garth intended to build. 'We may have more of a problem than we thought.'

'We've had problems since the day I offered for the place, but nothing that can't be overcome. First they claimed it was a famous beauty spot, though no one I spoke to had ever heard of it. Then they wanted to have the trees protected. Last week they burst into the council meeting and tried to stop me getting planning permission. But I got it anyway.'

'With some restrictions,' Bill pointed out. 'They may not look much, but they're going to cramp your style.'

'Not if I get them lifted, and I will. Trust me. I know the people to work on. So what is it this time?'

'Butterflies. The Outland is supposed to be the habitat of a rare breed.'

Garth groaned, muttering, 'Give me patience,' under his breath. Aloud he said, 'Stop worrying, Bill. If I wasn't put off by that bearded yob jabbing a placard in my eye and calling me a destroyer of creation, I think I can cope with a few butterflies.'

'I thought you should know that there's going to be a protest march at the Outland this afternoon. I tried to get the police to ban it, but no luck.'

'I wouldn't have done that, myself. It makes them look as if we're afraid of them.'

'Yes, but the television cameras will be there. It'll be on the news tonight.'

'Pity! But it can't do us any real harm. Thanks for letting me know, anyway.'

Later that afternoon Faye brought him a coffee and found him engrossed in the television screen.

'You always said watching the box in the afternoon was a dangerous habit,' she reminded him. 'According to you, it led to self-indulgence and time-wasting.'

'There's a news item that I need to see. I've taken an option on a strip of land and apparently a set of long-haired clowns are tramping over it, predicting the end of the world if I'm allowed to build there. There it is!'

The screen was occupied by a board, bearing the name Melkham Construction, set in an expanse of countryside.

Beside it stood an earnest young man addressing the camera.

'The protesters say that if this land falls victim to developers' frenzy it will be the destruction of a unique butterfly habitat—'

'Developers' frenzy,' Garth repeated angrily. 'I build houses for people to live in; people like that sanctimonious crowd. Where would they live if no one had built *their* homes? With the butterflies, I suppose! *GOOD GRIEF!*'

Startled, Faye followed his gaze and saw what had appalled him. The screen was filled with placards whose owners were hoisting them aloft, trying to catch the cameraman's eye. With an inward groan Faye saw that one of them was Kendall and right beside him, his face shining with enthusiasm, was Adrian. His placard bore the uncompromising words, GREED OUT, NATURE IN.

Garth turned accusing eyes on Faye. 'Did you know about this?'

'Of course I didn't. I knew Ken was going to some sort of ecology protest and Adrian begged to go with him. I think they mentioned the name Melkham, but I didn't connect it with you. You're Clayton Properties.'

'Melkham is a subsidiary. I acquired it last year.'

'Well, I didn't know that. Nor did Adrian.'

'I'll bet Kendall Haines knew, though. He must have loved getting my son to demonstrate against me in public.'

'Not everybody's mind is as tortuous as yours,' Faye said indignantly. 'Kendall is a decent, straightforward man. He'd never pull a stunt like that.'

'I wonder.'

'Garth, you're being impossible. Kendall fights for

what he believes in and so does Adrian. You should be proud of your son. He's one of life's dragon slayers. How was he to know that you were the dragon? He'd be interested to find out.'

'And if I don't tell him, I'm sure you will.'

'Goodness, no! I won't say a word. You must deal with this in your own way. But go carefully. Your son is no fool.'

At the end of the afternoon she drove to the Pattersons' to collect Cindy and Barker. Cindy chattered non-stop about her day but, as soon as she was home, she ran to her father to say it all again. Garth hugged her and Faye was relieved to see that his mood had improved. Barker had vanished to the kitchen, to be lovingly scolded for his muddy paws and fed some of his favourite buttered scones.

'Can we go out and play ball with Barker?' Cindy begged when she was sure she hadn't deprived Daddy of a single detail.

'I thought he'd been chasing around a garden all day.'

'Yes, but it's a very posh garden with lots of potted plants—'

'Oh, heavens!' Faye groaned.

'It wasn't Barker's fault. He didn't mean to knock it over, and he didn't know it was a prize bush.'

'No wonder Mr Patterson looked a bit tense when he said goodbye.'

'It's his own fault,' Garth observed. 'He should have known better than to leave his prize bush around when Barker was there.'

Cindy flung him a grateful look. 'Anyway, Barker wants to run and run in his own garden.'

'Can't you play with him?'

'You can throw the ball further than me. I'll go and get it.' She scampered off.

'Better get two,' Garth called. 'You know he always loses one.'

'Thanks, Daddy.' Her voice faded down the hall.

'I've got a pile of bookkeeping work to do,' Faye protested to thin air.

'Mummy!' came Cindy's imperious voice before Faye could answer. 'Barker wants to *play*.'

Garth grinned wickedly. 'Go on,' he told her. 'You've got your orders. That dog wants to play, and his social secretary is going to make sure everyone jumps to attention.'

'*Mummy—*'

'Coming, coming!'

Faye obediently headed for the garden and threw the ball for half an hour. Although she was annoyed with Garth, she had to admit he was spot on about Cindy. Nothing mattered to the little girl except giving her four-pawed darling whatever he wanted. She smiled with pleasure at the sight of child and dog romping together in perfect understanding.

Then her smile faded into a frown at something she thought she'd seen. She watched Barker carefully and wondered if his back legs really were a little stiff, or was she imagining it? Then he went bounding down the garden after a ball, charging through a tall heap of twigs Fred had just finished gathering up. Fred's little dance of rage and the terrible threats he hurled at Barker's retreating form made her double up with laughter, and the matter passed from her mind.

Adrian arrived home two hours later, full of delight over his day but, to Faye's relief, minus the placard. As she'd promised Garth, she kept quiet about what she knew.

Garth seemed to have forgotten his annoyance. He asked Adrian about his afternoon and listened attentively to his replies. Faye watched a flush of pleasure come to the boy's face. To have his father showing interest in his concerns was an unexpected delight.

'It was great, Dad. We were on telly.'

'I know. I saw you. In fact, I taped it for you to see.'

Adrian beamed. 'Great! Can we see it now?'

Garth put the video tape in and they watched it together.

'That placard is good,' Garth said. 'Greed out. Nature in. Who thought of it?'

'It was Kendall's idea. He's really brilliant at that sort of thing. He says firms like Melkham are nothing but selfish, greedy predators, and they have to be fought in any way you can.'

'Has he got any good ideas about fighting them?'

'Yes, 'cos he knows something they don't.'

'What's that?'

'That bit of land is covered by a special planning act. If anyone wants to build on it they have to comply with special conditions, and they have to do it by a certain date. If they don't, they lose the chance.'

'And that date's coming up?' Garth asked in a neutral voice.

'Next Wednesday. Then Ken's going to court to say they can't do it, because the date's past.'

'That's really clever of him. But suppose Melkham knows about it?'

'Kendall says they can't do, because they'd have done something by now. He says we're going to take them completely by surprise.'

'But shouldn't Melkham's point of view be considered?' Garth asked seriously. 'After all, people need somewhere to live, as well as butterflies.'

'Kendall says it doesn't have to be there,' Adrian explained earnestly. 'Besides, it's not just houses. Melkham is going to build a shopping complex and an office block, because that's where the real money is.'

Garth became acutely aware that his wife was watching him from the doorway and at this pronouncement her eyebrows gave a cynical lift.

'How do you know that?' Garth demanded after a moment.

'Because Kendall says so.'

'But no plans have been pub— That is—he can't be certain what Melkham intends unless he's seen plans.'

'Kendall says he doesn't have to see them. He says he knows shops and offices have got to be there, because it won't be fi—' Adrian hesitated and spoke the next words slowly, 'financially viable without them. And he says the man behind it all never does anything except for money.'

'But perhaps he's got that wrong,' Garth suggested, a slight edge on his voice.

'I don't think so,' Adrian said, frowning. 'Kendall knows everything. He says—'

'Yes, fine,' Garth interrupted him restively. He felt he might do something desperate if he had to hear any more of what 'Kendall said'.

Cindy bounded in, full of delight over her brother's television appearance, and the two of them went away together to tell Barker all about it. Faye remained in the doorway, watching her husband's brooding face. At last he looked up and their eyes met.

'Shops and offices, huh?' she echoed mockingly. 'Fancy that!'

'You know nothing about how these things are done,' he growled.

'But Kendall does, doesn't he? That's why you really hate him, because he's the one person you can't fool.'

'Rubbish! It's because he's stealing my son. He's going to be very sorry about that. Adrian's having a foot in both camps can work for me, as well as against me.'

'Garth, if you make use of what that child has just told you, he'll never speak to you again,' Faye said in alarm.

'Sentimental nonsense! The sooner he learns about the real world the better.'

'And what do you think he'll do? The moment he knows what you're up to, he'll warn Kendall.'

'Don't you understand? It doesn't make any difference. Let Kendall know that I've found out. He can't stop me.'

'All right,' Faye said quietly. 'Go ahead. Use what you learned today to defeat Kendall. Let Adrian find out that you tricked him into betraying his friend. Then get yourself another son, because you'll have lost this one for ever.'

'I'm not that much of a fool. I won't alienate Adrian, but I can't just let it go at this. I've got too much money tied up in that site.'

'Then why didn't you check the legal position before you bought it?'

'I have lawyers whose job it is to do just that and, believe me, heads will roll.' He rose from the sofa. 'I'm going to make some phone calls in the study.'

Faye returned to work at her computer, trying to shrug mentally and tell herself that if Garth wanted to make his son totally disillusioned with him, it wasn't her fault. Perhaps Adrian really did need to discover how low his father could sink.

But the thought of the little boy's pain kept intruding and made it impossible to concentrate. His unhappy face was there before her inner eye, but it kept getting mixed up with Garth's face. Her husband was heading for disaster and he couldn't see it. But when it was too late and Adrian wanted nothing more to do with him, then his suffering would begin.

It was his own fault, her reasonable mind argued. He'd put their marriage on the basis of a business deal. It was time he learned the true cost of business.

If only her heart could be reasonable! It ached for her child's pain, and somehow Garth's pain was in there too, complicating everything.

She worked late, forcing herself to concentrate on figures that meant nothing beside her inner turmoil. At last she got up and went downstairs. She must make at least one more effort to help Garth see what he was doing.

But the study was in darkness. Faye could hear movement coming from his little monastic bedroom, but she stopped with her hand on the knob. Garth slept naked and, however much they'd quarrelled in the past, the sight of his head on the pillow, tousled and vulnerable-looking, had always been able to melt her heart. She couldn't bring herself to go in there.

Guiltily she realized that she'd been too preoccupied to notice the passage of time and she hadn't said goodnight to the children. She looked in on Adrian, kissed him in his sleep and crept out. But she could hear a soft murmuring from Cindy's room, as though the child was talking to someone.

'I thought so,' she said, looking around the door.

Barker was sprawled on the bed, contending with Cindy for the available space. 'Out, dog!' she commanded. 'No sleeping in here!'

Barker eyed her, and stayed where he was.

'Off!' Faye insisted, pointing to the door.

'Oh, please let him stay, Mummy,' Cindy begged.

'Not a chance. Apart from the fact that it's unhygienic, where would you sleep? You're clinging on to the edge as it is.'

'I don't mind clinging on to the edge—'

'Cindy, I'm not arguing about this. Barker has to go. Come along, make him get off.'

Cindy slid her toes beneath Barker and wriggled them, which was usually enough to make him jump down. Not this time. Cindy wriggled her toes again, but he only regarded her reproachfully. She wriggled harder, and he merely settled down more deeply.

'He doesn't want to,' Cindy said unarguably. 'It took him ages to get up. He walked around and around the bed as if he wasn't sure he could do it.'

'Oh, you are an awkward animal!' Faye sighed, putting her arms around him and heaving. Barker tried to take root, but the bedspread was slippery and he slid helplessly off onto the floor. He landed heavily and let out a squeal of pain.

'Mummy, Mummy, you hurt him!' Cindy said, jumping out of bed and throwing her arms about Barker's neck. 'You hurt him, you hurt him,' she repeated in tears.

'Darling, I didn't mean to,' Faye protested, almost as distressed as the child, for Barker was now making a pitiful wailing noise. 'Oh, you poor old boy! What did I do? I'm so sorry.'

Garth and Adrian came in, alerted by the noise.

Adrian tried to entice the dog to his feet with a titbit, but Barker seemed unable to move, even for food. That was when they knew something was really wrong.

'Mummy!' Cindy cried hysterically.

'All right, I know who can help,' Faye assured her.

Garth followed her into her bedroom, but when she reached for the telephone he stopped her. 'Who are you calling?'

'Kendall. He's a vet.'

'Barker is registered with an excellent animal hospital.'

'But it's late at night. He's in pain. He can't wait until morning.'

'He won't have to. They have a night service. I'll call them.'

'And take the poor animal there in the car, when he's like this? Oh, no! If I call Ken he'll come and see him here.'

He seized her wrist, his eyes blazing. 'Faye, that man is my enemy and hell will freeze over before I ask him for help, let alone have him in this house. I'll call the vet and get someone out here.'

He made the call at once and after a few moments handed Faye the phone. 'You'd better explain,' he said.

Faye described what had happened and the night duty vet, a pleasant-sounding woman called Miss McGeorge, said, 'That sounds familiar. If I'm right it's not serious, but I'll know more when I've seen him. Expect me in ten minutes.'

'She's coming,' Faye said as she hung up.

'So there's no need for your friend.'

'As it happens, no!' She eyed him accusingly. 'Would you really have let that poor dog suffer till morning rather than ask Kendall?'

'You obviously think I would.'

'Hell will freeze over—' she reminded him.

'Look, I don't know what I'd have done.'

'Even for Cindy?'

'I told you, I don't know,' he snapped.

Miss McGeorge arrived soon, listened to the story, then gently coaxed Barker to his feet.

'His back legs seemed a little stiff this afternoon,' Faye said self-reproachfully. 'I wish I'd called you then, but I wasn't quite sure.'

Miss McGeorge took hold of one of Barker's back legs and waggled it slightly. From under the thick fur came the sound of a sharp crack.

'Just as I thought,' she said. 'He's got a touch of arthritis. It tends to happen to elderly dogs.'

'Can you make it go away?' Cindy asked anxiously.

'I can make his pain go away,' Miss McGeorge promised. 'I can't cure the arthritis, but I'll give him an injection that will make it stop hurting for tonight. Bring him to the surgery on Monday and I'll decide what pills he needs.'

Her cheerful manner had its effect and soon after she'd given the injection and departed, Barker was visibly better. The children coaxed him back to his basket, settled him for the night and were finally persuaded to return to bed.

Faye slept for an hour, then instinct prompted her to rise and go quietly downstairs to the place where Barker's basket was kept.

'And what are you two doing down here?' she asked unnecessarily.

Two small faces looked up guiltily, then quickly assumed innocent expressions.

'We were checking that he's all right, Mummy,' Adrian said, adding cheekily, 'Just like you.'

Cindy tactfully smothered her giggle and Faye said, 'All right, funny man, how is he?'

'He's just been out into the garden,' Cindy said. 'I think he's all right.'

'What's going on?' Garth asked sleepily, appearing in his dressing gown.

They all explained and he knelt down to scratch the invalid's head. Cindy and Adrian offered biscuits, which were accepted, and Garth observed, 'He's going to make the most of this.'

'Daddy,' Cindy reproached him. 'That's not kind.'

'It's a plain statement of fact. Now his pain's gone he's loving the attention.'

'But you will take him back to the vet for his pills?' she asked worriedly.

'Of course I will.'

'He means that *I* will,' Faye said lightly. 'Daddy has to be at work.'

Garth shrugged. 'If we can set off first thing, I don't mind being an hour late.'

The children looked gratified and Adrian said, 'Thanks for calling the vet, Daddy. Is it very expensive if they come out late?'

'Never mind that.'

'But I can help, from my pocket money.'

'So can I,' Cindy volunteered eagerly.

Garth ruffled her hair. 'You've already had next week's in advance, both of you. You're too young to start getting into debt. Let me take care of Barker.'

Adrian grinned. 'Thanks, Dad.'

Garth grinned back and suddenly they looked uncannily alike, although they didn't share a single feature.

For one brief moment there was understanding between them. Then it passed and they both became self-conscious.

'Off to bed, now,' Garth said.

Faye tried to catch his eye and send him the silent message, 'See how much you've gained. Don't risk losing it.' But then she realized that he was determined not to look at her and she turned away, heavy-hearted.

He was as good as his word, going to work late on Monday morning in order to chauffeur Barker to the vet. But that night he returned home later than ever and Faye guessed that it was the legal challenge over the Outland that took up so much time.

She even considered calling Kendall herself to warn him what was in the wind. But, as Garth had said, it was already too late, and it would have felt uneasily like conspiring with Kendall against the man who was still her husband.

All Tuesday she was braced for a call from Kendall, angry because Garth had met the deadline. But Tuesday passed into Wednesday and Kendall didn't telephone either herself or Adrian. She couldn't raise the subject with Garth, as he'd stayed at his office over Tuesday night.

On Wednesday afternoon she returned from school with the children to find a message from Kendall on her answer machine, telling them to watch the local news. There was no more information and it was hard to tell from his voice whether he was pleased or disappointed.

The very first item on the news was about the Outland and there was Kendall, smiling and talking about a significant victory.

'Now that the deadline has passed we have no more

to fear from Melkham Construction,' he said. 'This is a great day for the countryside.'

An announcer appeared on the screen. 'Melkham, of course, is no more than a wholly owned subsidiary of Clayton Properties, the fast growing empire of Garth Clayton. We tried to contact Mr Clayton to ask how he felt about being beaten to the post, but he wasn't available for comment...'

Adrian turned slowly and stared at Faye. 'He means Daddy, doesn't he?'

'That's right,' Faye said. She sat very still, knowing that she was the only one who'd heard Garth's arrival. She was aware of him crossing the hall to stand just outside the open door, listening to every word.

'But— I told him—' Adrian stammered. 'I gave the whole game away— He could have—' He paled as he realized the full implications.

'Yes, he could have made use of what you said,' Faye agreed. 'But that would have been dishonourable, and your father wouldn't do it.'

''Course he wouldn't,' Cindy said scornfully to her brother. 'Daddy would never do anything mean or dis—dishorrible!'

Adrian was deep in thought. 'Mummy,' he said at last, 'Uncle Ken is one of the good guys, isn't he?'

'Definitely.'

'And Daddy's quite different to Uncle Ken. But Daddy's one of the good guys too.' His forehead creased. 'Isn't he?'

'There's more than one kind of good guy,' Faye explained. 'There's Uncle Ken's kind, and Daddy's kind. But they're both good.'

Out of the corner of her eye she saw Garth back away into the shadows. She longed to talk to him, to tell him how happy she was that he'd put his son's feelings before his profits. But that must wait.

A moment later the front door opened and closed noisily and Garth's cheerful call of 'Where is everyone?' made Cindy and Adrian rush into the hall. Cindy threw herself joyously into his arms. Adrian held off a little, studying his father with a puzzled frown. But at last he, too, snuggled against him.

Nobody mentioned the matter until the children were going to bed. Then Adrian looked Garth full in the face and said quietly, 'Thanks, Dad.'

'You can always trust me,' Garth said, returning his son's gaze.

Adrian nodded before mounting the stairs with Cindy. He didn't speak but, as he turned away, Faye just glimpsed his smile.

'Thank you from me, too,' she said, laying a hand on Garth's arm.

He looked elated, as he'd sometimes looked before when he'd found the key to a tricky situation.

'It should be me thanking you,' he said. 'I was about to make the biggest blunder of all time and you stopped me. I'm grateful, and for the things you said to them about me. I appreciate fair dealing.'

There was something not quite right in his voice, a hint of calculation that troubled her. But she tried again.

'I hate you and Kendall being enemies—'

'In the circumstances, we could hardly be anything else.'

'But couldn't we say that the battle's finally over?'

His air of elation was undimmed. 'Of course it's not over. It's just moved into a new phase. I know my enemy now. He's a subtle man and I was blundering about. But not any more. Now I've learned subtlety too.'

'And just what does that mean?'

'You can hardly expect me to tell you when you have one foot in the enemy camp.'

'Meaning you don't trust me?' she asked, letting her hand fall away from him. 'Despite our differences, I think I've earned better than that from you, Garth.'

'I told you, I appreciate your coming to my defence just now. You're a decent person, Faye, I know that. It's just that I never entirely trust my business partners. Now, I have a lot of work to do. Unless you want me for something?'

'Not a thing,' she assured him in a toneless voice.

CHAPTER SEVEN

'DADDY, you will look after poor Barker, won't you?'

'I've already promised I will.'

'Yes, but *really*?'

'Really. My word on it.'

It was time for Cindy and Adrian to go to the school camp in Cornwall but, on the morning of departure, Cindy had qualms about leaving her friend.

'He's not very well,' she explained for the tenth time. 'He was limping last night and I think his legs are hurting again.'

'Then I'll take him to the vet,' Garth assured her.

'This morning?'

'This morning.'

'You won't make him wait?'

'Cindy, get into the car!'

'But you won't make him wait, will you?'

'I won't make him wait.'

'You're sure?'

'I'm sure.'

'*Sure* sure?'

'Cindy, I'll take him to the vet.' Garth was beginning to sound frazzled.

'Promise?'

'Get into the car.'

'*Promise?*'

Garth tore his hair. 'I promise, I promise. Now, *get into the car*, both of you, or we'll be late and they'll go without you.'

But she couldn't depart without reassuring Barker that he would be all right because Daddy had promised.

'Cindy, I'm leaving in exactly one minute,' Garth said, at the end of his tether. 'With you or without you.'

Both children kissed Faye and scrambled into the car. As they drove away Faye was sure she could hear Cindy's voice faintly, saying, 'Daddy, you're sure you won't forget…?'

She enjoyed a private chuckle. As Garth had said, he was handling his task with subtlety. He'd even gone to watch Adrian playing football. His team had made it to the final of the inter-schools trophy and the whole family had been there for Adrian's big day.

Everyone had enjoyed it enormously, and when Cindy had kissed her father goodnight at the foot of the stairs she'd whispered, 'Thank you for coming, Daddy. You made it really special.'

'Hey, what about Mummy?' he'd queried. 'She was there too.'

'That's different. Mummy's always there.'

Faye had overheard this exchange from the kitchen and had come out, smiling quizzically at Garth.

'Don't take that the wrong way,' he'd said hastily.

'How should I take it?'

'She didn't mean to put you down.' Through his awkwardness she had detected the attempt at kindness.

'I didn't take it that way. Garth, Cindy has just said the nicest thing about me that any child can say about a parent. I promise you, I don't feel put down.'

'The nicest thing—?' She'd watched as comprehension dawned on his face. 'She said you're always there. Yes—yes, I see.' He'd sounded heavy, and she'd felt a stirring of pity for him. He was trying so hard, but something constantly eluded him.

Now it was the great day of departure for Cornwall. Garth returned from dropping off Cindy and Adrian, looking weary. 'I watched the coach go and Cindy was at the window, mouthing "Barker" at me,' he said.

'Don't worry, I've called the vet. His appointment is in an hour.'

'Faye—actually—'

'I'll take him,' she said, smiling.

'Thanks. And by the way, before I go, will you make a date in your diary for next Monday, at noon? I'm having a press function for the anniversary range and I need you there.'

'You mean I've got to meet journalists and talk to them?'

'It's no big deal. It's not the proper launch. That will be on the exact date of our anniversary. This is a kind of teaser, to let the property press get a hint of what's in store. We'll have models of the houses on display. I'll give you some booklets about them in advance, so that you can discuss them knowledgeably.'

'I'm just kind of shy about being on show,' she demurred.

'But you promised to help me out,' he reminded her, 'and this is the sort of thing I need you to do.'

'Of course it is,' she said, pulling herself together. 'Don't worry, I'll turn up and do my stuff.'

'Great. And buy a new outfit. The best of everything.'

'So that when they look at me they'll say, "Boy, must he be doing well if she can afford to dress like that!"'

He grinned. 'You're developing a real talent for this.

Miss McGeorge examined Barker thoroughly and said his painkillers weren't quite strong enough. She prescribed some different pills and gave him the first one immediately. By that afternoon he was moving more easily and by early evening he was as mischievous as ever.

'I see he's back to normal,' Garth observed when he returned. 'Down, boy! This suit's just been cleaned.'

'The vet gave him stronger pills,' Faye said. 'I think they're doing the trick.'

'Good.'

'But it'll be a few days before we're certain. I've made another appointment—'

'You're doing a great job, Faye. Now, I've got a pile of work to get on with—'

'But you need to know all this. *You're* supposed to be caring for Barker.'

'Of course, and I promise you I'm taking it very seriously. But you can brief me later. Tell Nancy to bring me a snack in the study, will you?'

'But Cindy will—'

'By the way, I brought this home for you.' He handed her a thick folder. 'It'll tell you everything about the anniversary range.' He vanished.

Faye glared at his study door, then sighed. When she'd spoken to Nancy she returned to studying a list of traditional anniversary gifts.

'Paper after the first year,' she mused. 'He gave me a book that I'd been longing for. It was terribly expensive, and he starved himself to pay for it. The next year it was cotton and he gave me that lovely summer housecoat. The third year, leather—that was a shoulder bag—'

How his eyes had shone as he offered his gifts to her! How happy he'd been when she was pleased! She drew a breath and firmly dismissed the memory.

At last came the call from the children to say they'd arrived safely. Adrian told her all about the journey, before saying, 'Cindy's here and she—' His voice faded, there was a slight scuffle and Adrian hissed, 'Let me finish, you little brat.'

Then Cindy's voice. 'Hello, Mummy.'

'Hello, darling. Is it nice in camp?'

'It's super. Mummy, how's Barker? Did Daddy take him to the vet? What happened? Is he any better?'

'Just a minute.' Faye pressed a switch to connect the call to Garth's study, and walked in.

'Pick up the phone,' she said. 'Cindy wants to talk to you.'

She stayed there while he answered. She could tell that the little girl must have launched straight into her favourite topic. Garth became slightly defensive, while trying to sound in control.

'Yes, darling, of course I took— That is, Barker's been to the vet and he's much better— Well, because the vet gave him stronger pills,' he finished, repeating Faye's words. From his frown it was clear that he was trying to recall the rest.

'They seem to be working,' he continued gamely, 'but it'll take a few days to be sure— Well, on his next appointment— That's right, he's booked in for—'

He signalled wildly to Faye, who mouthed, 'Next week.'

'Next week,' he repeated into the phone. 'The exact day? I forget—' He appealed silently to Faye, but she shook her head and backed out.

Listening from the hall, she had to admit that he improvised pretty well for a man who didn't know what he was talking about. But the way he slammed the phone down made his feelings clear.

'I suppose you've been standing out here, enjoying yourself,' he grunted, emerging from the study.

'Don't blame me,' she said impishly. 'I tried to give you a full briefing earlier, but you were too busy to listen.'

'So you landed me in it.'

'You landed yourself in it. After all, you know the saying.'

'No, I don't, but I'm sure you're going to have fun telling me.'

'If you can't do the time, don't do the crime.'

'What?'

'If you can't keep the promise, don't make it. If you want to take the credit, you've got to put in the work. Cindy asked you to care for Barker, not me, because it matters to her that *you* should do it.' She smiled at him cheekily. 'So do it.'

'Thanks! Thanks a lot!'

He would have died sooner than let her suspect that she'd startled him, not only with her challenge but in what she'd learned about tough dealing. As a tough dealer himself he respected that. He wondered where his wife had learned all these disconcerting lessons.

Faye finally bought herself a matching blue silk coat and dress. It cost a fortune and looked it, which she knew would satisfy her husband. On the whole she was pleasantly surprised by her own appearance.

She rejected his offer to send his chauffeur-driven car for her and drove herself there. A parking space had been reserved for her. Doors opened at her approach and she was instantly conducted to the top floor, where Garth reigned.

She was interested to see his new London premises, which he'd acquired since their parting. She found them much as she'd expected, quietly luxurious and efficient.

Money had been spent, but not on frills. Garth got value from every penny.

As she stepped out of the lift an overpoweringly gracious young woman was waiting for her. Faye knew at once that this could only be Lysandra. Everything about her fitted the superior voice she'd heard on the telephone. Lysandra was tall and slender, dressed in an elegant charcoal business suit. With her shoulder-length red hair and gold accessories, she looked stunning. Faye had felt stylish until that moment, but next to the super-chic Lysandra she could sense herself retreating into dowdiness.

'Good morning, Mrs Clayton,' she said, advancing with her hand outstretched. 'I'm Lysandra Bates, Mr Clayton's Director of Publicity. We've all been looking forward so much to meeting you.'

'We?' Faye asked, surprised.

'Everyone in the Publicity Department. It's such a coup for us to have you part of the campaign.' Her tone implied that Faye had no other existence.

'Mr Clayton said you were a little hesitant at first, but I was sure you'd be glad you agreed when you knew how much this mattered to us,' Lysandra continued. She led the way into a room that was luxuriously furnished with pale grey leather armchairs, offering her tea, coffee. Nothing could have been more gracious or deferential than her manner, yet Faye detected a faint hint of contempt. This smooth, beautiful young woman had sized her up and found her wanting.

Garth appeared and greeted Faye with a polite smile and a kiss on the cheek. She responded in the same way. They were like two actors performing their roles perfectly on cue.

'Lysandra will show you the models and explain

everything,' he said. 'The press will start to arrive in about an hour.'

'Everything is quite ready,' Lysandra told him. 'Press packs, free samples—'

Faye attempted a mild joke. 'You give free samples of houses?'

Lysandra's laughter managed to combine weary courtesy, exaggerated patience and restrained derision in equal measure. 'Naturally not. But there are many smaller items, which the construction press appreciate. It's part of my job to know them all personally and to select free gifts to suit the individual.'

'I'm sure you've covered every detail admirably,' Garth told her. 'You never let me down.'

Unlike his wife, Faye thought.

'I try not to,' Lysandra told him with a smile that excluded Faye. 'I'll fetch you when they're all assembled.'

'Come into my office as soon as it's over,' Garth said. 'We have a lot to discuss.'

Faye was about to say that she preferred to leave at once when she realized he was talking to his beautiful assistant. When he did address her it was to say, 'Lysandra will look after you. Leave everything in her splendid hands.'

He disappeared.

'It's this way,' Lysandra said, pointing across the corridor. Faye followed her and found herself in a huge corner room with windows on two sides. Six other people, power-dressed women and men in business suits, were already there, crowding around something in the centre. Lysandra introduced them as members of the Publicity Department, and showed Faye what they were looking at. On a large display plinth stood six models of houses, each one about two feet wide by eighteen inches high.

'These are our very newest designs, and top secret at the moment,' Lysandra explained. She flashed Faye a beaming smile, revealing small, perfectly white teeth. 'Not secret from you, of course.' Everyone laughed at this witticism. Faye smiled.

'There are two for those with more modest incomes, two for the executive class, and these two are de luxe,' she continued smoothly. 'And you'll be delighted to know that we've finally managed to find the right name for them.'

'How thrilling!' Faye said.

'Yes, isn't it? It's going to be called the Diamond Range. We all had to put our thinking caps on but, with it being your tenth anniversary, of course the name had been staring us in the face all the time.'

Any minute now she's going to pat me on the head, Faye thought. Aloud, she said, 'I'm afraid I don't see the connection with my wedding anniversary.'

'Your *tenth* wedding anniversary,' Lysandra corrected gently. 'The time when husbands give their wives diamond jewellery. That's why we've called this the Diamond Range.' She said the last words slowly, as if to an idiot.

'But there's some mistake,' Faye said. 'The tenth anniversary gift is tin or aluminium. Diamonds are for the sixtieth.'

Lysandra's perfect smile barely wavered. 'I think not,' she said sweetly. 'I have the list here.'

Faye studied it with bewilderment, unable to recognize anything. Instead of the traditional paper, cotton, leather of the first three years, she read clocks, china, and crystal.

'Fourth—appliances?' she said. 'The fourth was always fruit and flowers. And the fifth was wood, but here it says silverware.'

'I see what's happened,' Lysandra said with a forgiving smile. 'You're thinking of the old list, but we work from the one that came in about fifteen years ago. The tenth anniversary is diamond jewellery. Naturally Mr Clayton will be giving you diamonds. In fact, we've already selected some pieces for your approval.'

'We?' Faye asked.

'Mr Clayton relies on me for everything,' Lysandra said coolly. 'I was able to suggest some diamond pieces that might be suitable, since you were—er—unavailable for consultation. Perhaps you'd care to inspect them now.'

Too dazed to protest, Faye looked on as Lysandra produced several black velvet trays on which sparkled earrings, necklaces, rings and bracelets. They were beautiful, but she felt no pleasure. They seemed like the very essence of everything that had gone wrong between herself and Garth.

'They're lovely, aren't they?' Lysandra cooed. 'So much better than tin, so I'm sure you'll feel you've gained by the exchange.'

'But I don't,' Faye said defiantly. 'I just think it's sad to throw away the old traditions.'

'Old traditions are so sweet,' Lysandra said, 'but not very functional.'

'And your list is very functional, isn't it?'

'Oh, it's been an immense help to people like us in the construction industry.'

People like us. She was talking about herself and Garth.

'But it's so false,' Faye said helplessly.

'False?'

'Artificial. This isn't the real anniversary list. It's just a way of selling more washing machines.'

'The modern customer demands appliances already installed in a new house—'

'Fine, then do that. But don't pretend it has anything to do with wedding anniversaries. I'm sorry, this just isn't what I agreed to help with.'

For the first time Lysandra was nonplussed. 'Well, if you'll—excuse me.' She hurried away, and returned a moment later with Garth.

'It had better be something important for you to have dragged me away from that meeting,' he said and, although he was speaking to Lysandra, Faye felt the words were directed at herself.

'We've got a problem,' she said, speaking pleasantly. 'I'm afraid I misunderstood why you wanted me. My fault, I dare say.'

'Well, I'm sure we can sort it out,' he said, also speaking with determined pleasantness.

'To me the tenth wedding anniversary means a gift of tin or aluminium, not diamonds. I didn't even know there was another list.'

'Well, surely you don't mind having diamonds?' he asked, frowning, and she knew he didn't really understand.

She shouldn't have started this, she thought. Why not just keep quiet and play her part? But some core of her, which had kept quiet too often in the past, insisted on standing firm.

'I do mind. If we're going to tie your new range in with our tenth wedding anniversary, then I think we should do it properly.'

'You're surely not suggesting that I give you tin?'

'It's what you're supposed to give,' she said stubbornly.

'Only from a sentimental point of view, surely?' Lysandra said. 'But this is a business decision. Mr Clayton and I have explored the matter from every angle and this decision offered optimum results.'

'Tin is the right thing,' Faye persisted. She met her husband's eyes, silently pleading with him, *Don't take her side against me. Say at least that you understand my point of view.*

But she knew Garth didn't understand a thing when she saw the anger flare in his eyes. He took her arm and drew her away from Lysandra, speaking in a soft, furious undervoice. 'If we'd still been living in a two-room flat it would be the right thing. But we've moved beyond that, in case you hadn't noticed. I'm a successful man, marketing a range of luxury houses for successful people. I can't celebrate that range with a tin plate. It would make me a laughing stock.'

'I'm sorry you feel that my standards make you a laughing stock, Garth, but that's the way I feel. I think you should do this without me.'

'You're a vital part of this promotion—'

'So why didn't you explain it to me properly?'

'I explained everything I thought needed explaining. I didn't know you were going to go off on this sentimental flight of fancy.'

'Thank you very much.'

He gritted his teeth. 'We'll talk about this tonight.'

'Tonight will be too late. I'd like to talk about it now.'

'Faye, don't do this to me, please. I've got a million things on my mind—'

'If I'm such a vital part of this, perhaps one of those things should be me.'

'All right, all right! I handled it clumsily. I'm sorry. Now can we just get on with this?'

'Without me.'

He was pale. 'You're not serious.'

'Garth, it never was a very good idea to put me in the press show. You and Miss Bates will handle everything perfectly together.'

Without another word she turned and walked out. Her head was up and she seemed calm, but inwardly she was seething with anger. As she reached the lift she heard a pattering of footsteps and turned to see Lysandra. When the lift doors opened Lysandra followed her in.

'What an unfortunate misunderstanding,' she said, smiling brightly. 'But I can assure you, Mrs Clayton, Garth didn't mean to upset you in any way.'

'I beg your pardon!' Faye said in frosty outrage.

'He doesn't always understand things the way we women do. Men aren't sentimental, are they? I promise you, Garth would be devastated to think—'

'How dare you?' Faye interrupted her fiercely. 'How dare you presume to explain my husband to me?'

'I assure you, I'm only—'

'You know nothing about him. *Nothing!*'

The lift had stopped. Faye stormed out and immediately pressed the button to make the doors close again. Her last view was of Lysandra gaping with astonishment.

Her fury sustained her all the way home but once there it began to seep away, to be replaced with weariness. The expensive silk clothes felt like an actor's costume for a role that was all wrong for her and she hurried to change them for dark green trousers and a pale yellow shirt. It was a lovely day and, with a linen jacket about her shoulders and flat shoes on her feet, she was ready for a stroll in the grounds.

'Come on,' she said to Barker. 'You're missing the children, aren't you?'

He padded amiably after her as she wandered into the trees. Faye threw the ball and was cheered to see him bound after it, obviously not in pain. But neither did he move with the vitality of a young dog and it brought home to her again how old he was. It was another reason for being angry with Garth.

'We're the same, you and me,' she said, sitting by the stream and fishing in her coat pocket for a biscuit. 'He's making use of us both to get what he wants. Underneath all his clever talk, that's the bottom line.' She stroked his ears. 'How's that for a mixed metaphor? What am I talking about? You wouldn't know a mixed metaphor if it jumped on you, not unless it was offering titbits.'

As if by a signal Barker began to sniff her coat. 'All right, here's a biscuit. Leave my fingers behind! What an idiot I was to make an issue of it! What else did I expect? We made a business deal and that's the only reason I'm here. Who cares what list he chose? It's all over between us, anyway.'

She settled herself more comfortably on the grass and stroked the furry head that was resting on her leg.

'You know who I was really mad at, don't you?' she mused. 'That woman. She acted as though she owned him. And she actually dared to explain him to me. To *me*! To his wife. I know him better than anyone. Oh, what does it matter? I'm not really his wife any more.'

She gave a sudden chuckle. 'But you should have heard me getting on my high horse with Lysandra. I've never done that before. Didn't know I could. That showed her. If you ask me, she sees herself as the next

Mrs Clayton.' Barker woofed agreement and eyed her coat significantly.

'OK, one more! But don't you dare suggest I'm jealous! She's welcome to him. It was just her being so rude that bothered me. Hey, I said *one*!'

They lingered together, enjoying the beautiful afternoon, until the sun began to set.

'Time to go in,' she said reluctantly. 'I'll bet he'll be home early tonight, and he'll have plenty to say to me.'

She was right. Garth arrived half an hour later and came looking for her. 'Can we talk?' he asked in an edgy voice.

'Yes. I'm sorry. It shouldn't have happened.'

'Whatever got into you to leave me with egg on my face like that? Everyone was expecting my wife to be there. I had to say you'd been taken ill. Are you going to do that on the big night?'

'No, of course not. The whole thing took me by surprise. I'd never heard of this other list. Why didn't you warn me?'

'I left everything to Lysandra. Besides, what difference does it make which list we use?'

She shrugged. 'None at all, I suppose.'

'You made a fool of me and I can't stand that. We had a bargain and you're not keeping it.'

'Garth, I'm sorry. What I did was—unprofessional, and I regret it.'

'Why, for heaven's sake? Why?'

'I told you, I was caught on the wrong foot. And that new list is horrible. You're only dragging me in because you think you'll sell more houses if you can make people feel warm and good. But there's nothing warm about washing machines. It's all so cynical.'

'I think I know best about marketing my own product.'

'You don't know much about families and these are supposed to be family homes—sorry, "product", since you have a problem with the idea of homes. You want to sell them to couples with children, people who love each other. Well, most wives and mothers would rather have a piece of tin given with love than all the diamonds in the world in this calculating way.'

'Tin! For Pete's sake!'

'I can remember when you didn't despise tin.'

'I can't.'

'Then it's your loss. When we were first married we ate off tin plates that we bought at a second-hand camping store. In fact, we didn't even buy them. You mended that man's boiler for free, and he gave us some things for the flat.'

'Oh, yes, and I felt ashamed because I'd started our marriage by failing you. I wanted to give you the moon and we ended up with stuff that nobody else wanted.'

'But I didn't care,' she said wildly. If only she could make him understand, even now. 'I was happy just to be with you. I thought you felt the same.'

'I was never happy until I could give you the nice things you deserved. I worked like a Trojan until I had enough for my own little builder's yard, and then a big yard. And then the sky was the limit. I did it for you and all you can do is hark back to the days when I had nothing to give you, because I was nobody.'

'You were somebody to me,' she cried. 'And to the children. But that wasn't enough for you. You've turned into such a different man.'

'Thank goodness!' he said abruptly.

'I'll never say that. I'll never stop mourning the man

I lost. He was all the world to me, but he went away and never came back.' She could see by his face that he didn't understand. They were strangers shouting in the dark, and a sudden burst of anguish made her cry, 'Oh, Garth, don't you remember?'

He was silent awhile before answering. 'Maybe my memories are different to yours,' he said at last, seeming to speak with difficulty. 'We obviously didn't find the same things important.'

'We thought we were together,' she said with a sigh. 'And we were travelling separate paths all along. And now here we are, in sight of the end.'

'Don't,' he said sombrely. 'Don't look back, Faye. We both know that's a mistake. We've each chosen our lives.'

There was a sadness in his face that she hadn't seen before. Suddenly she leaned over and kissed him. It was an impulse. She wasn't even sure what she wanted to come of it, except perhaps to evoke the old Garth, even if only fleetingly.

For a moment she thought it was happening. After a brief surprise he kissed her back, with a kind of yearning ache. She could feel him trembling, though whether with passion or emotion she wasn't sure. She tightened her arms, seeking to reach the part of him that lived behind the proud barrier. Her strong resolutions vanished. If only she could still touch his heart...

'Garth,' she whispered in a pleading voice, 'try to remember...' He lifted his head to search her face. She could see his eyes and read their trouble and confusion. Then he tensed and broke free from her.

'This isn't a good idea, Faye. You were right all along about it being over.'

'Yes,' she stammered. 'Yes I was...'

'There's nothing for us now but to see this through to the end and say goodbye.' A shudder went through him. 'So, for pity's sake, let's get it over with quickly.'

CHAPTER EIGHT

WITH a clash of cymbals the orchestra brought the symphony to an end. The conductor turned to receive the well-earned applause. Faye came out of her happy trance. The music had been magnificent and she was reluctant to return to reality with all its problems and confusions.

It was late in the evening, but while the children were at camp she needn't rush home. For their sakes Garth had often managed to return early, but during their absence he'd reverted to staying late at the office. It was as though he and Faye were holding their breaths in this delicate situation.

Daydreaming, she left the concert hall without looking where she was going, and collided with someone. 'I'm terribly sorry, I— *Kendall!*'

'Hello, darling.' He kissed her cheek.

'Where did you appear from?' she asked, smiling.

'I was at the concert. Come and have a drink with me.'

It was a fine evening and they found a pub with tables outside in the garden, and coloured lights hanging from the trees. Kendall bought cider for himself, orange juice for Faye and hot dogs for both of them.

'Fancy you going to a classical concert,' Faye said. 'Where were you sitting?'

After an awkward pause Kendall said, 'All right, I didn't actually go to the concert. I knew you'd be there because I was with you when you bought the ticket, ages ago. I waited outside.'

It was nice to know that he was so eager to see her, but the little lie troubled her. Then she determinedly pushed it out of her head.

'I've missed you,' Kendall said.

'And I you.'

'Well, there's always the television,' he said, speaking apparently lightly but with a significant edge.

'Television?'

'Last night. What did you think?'

With a gasp of dismay she remembered that Kendall had been on a talk show, due to be broadcast the previous evening.

'It's all right,' he said, reading her face. 'I don't suppose you could watch it with him around.'

She wasn't fooled by his easy tone. Kendall had a touch of vanity about his media appearances. Faye had always found this slightly endearing and had fondly made much of him, while he basked in her admiration. She knew she ought to make amends now by inventing a convincing excuse, but suddenly she was too tired for white lies and the truth came out before she could think properly.

'Kendall, I'm sorry, Garth wasn't even in last night. But I've got so much on my mind just now—'

'That you didn't give me a thought. Fair enough.' He spoke with a kind of determined brightness that set her at a distance.

'Kendall, please—'

'Forget it. I'm sure you're having a very difficult time. Is your husband making life hard?'

'Not really. He's behaving well to the children. It's lovely to see him with Cindy. She just basks in his attention. And he's doing better with Adrian, too. But I worry that he's just using them.'

'I suppose he might have honestly seen the light. Perhaps he's afraid of a lonely old age.' Kendall shrugged. 'I should think he's certainly heading for one.'

'Garth's not afraid of anything. He's got too much self-confidence. He's— Oh, I don't how how to say it—'

It was useless trying to define Garth. The more she tried, the more he slipped through her fingers. She could describe his manner and his infuriating behaviour. But there were no words for his sudden grin, full of devilment and charm, or the wild wonderment of his dreams. Once he'd shared those dreams with her and it had been like watching shooting stars. But that was a long time ago.

She gave up, remembering that it irked Kendall to hear too much about Garth. 'Tell me how things are with you,' she said.

'There's not a lot going on in my life at the moment,' he said. 'I work, and I think of you.'

'Have you finished your book yet?'

'I told you I had, at the football match.'

'Oh, yes, you did. Sorry, I forgot. Are you happy with it?'

'I'm never happy with my writing, you know that.'

'Yes, you were always changing things until the last minute.'

She persevered with the theme of his writing, conscientiously asking all the right questions, until the subject was exhausted. She searched for another one then realized, with dismay, what she was doing. She and Kendall had always found plenty to talk about. Yet tonight something was wrong. The air didn't vibrate with excitement as it did when Garth was around.

But she wasn't her usual self at the moment, she remembered with relief. When things returned to normal everything would be well between them again. But try as she might, she couldn't find the elusive spark that would bring her alive in Kendall's company.

'It's very late,' she said at last. 'I should be getting home now.'

'I'll walk you to your car.'

She tucked her hand in his arm and everything was comfortable between them, as it had always been. But it was no longer enough. When they reached the car she said, almost desperately, 'Kiss me goodnight.'

Kendall's embrace was the same as always but his kiss didn't thrill her, and now she wondered if it ever really had.

'Faye...' Kendall said tensely.

'Kiss me again,' she pleaded.

'Better not. Your thoughts were wandering. Like I told you, it has to be all or nothing with me. Goodnight, Faye.'

As she went through the front door Faye could hear Garth's voice from behind his study door, sounding as though he was on the phone. She was glad, as she couldn't bear to talk. She went up the stairs, straight to her own room.

A shower made her feel better. Wrapping a soft towelling dressing gown about her she returned to the bedroom and switched off all the lights except a soft lamp by her dressing table. Her mind was in turmoil.

Something had been different tonight and Kendall had recognized it too. It was all because of Garth. He'd kissed her that first night and her body had responded out of sheer surprise. If she'd been more prepared she might have stilled those treacherous impulses. But she hadn't stilled them and the memories had remained. They had prompted her to reach out to him on the evening after the disastrous press show. But he hadn't wanted her. They'd grown too far apart. There was an ache of desolation in her heart.

She remembered the lithe firmness of Garth's body and how good it felt to hold it. He'd been a generous as well as a skilful lover, warm and tender and eager for her pleasure as well as his own.

She knew it was dangerous to dwell on these memories, but they were part of the happiest time of her life. The fulfilment hadn't just been physical. Garth's love had filled the world, making her feel valued and totally a woman. Without her even knowing it, a smile touched her lips. Then it faded into a sigh.

She was so absorbed in her reverie that she didn't see the door open and Garth enter quietly. He stood watching her, his eyes darkening with anger at the look of tender introspection on her face. She thought she was alone, so it wasn't teasing that made her lips curl in that sweet smile as if she was thinking of something—or someone—who made her blissfully happy.

Suddenly she seemed to become aware of him and turned her head. 'You shouldn't be here,' she said.

'I wanted to talk to you.' He looked like a man under terrible strain, and his eyes were haggard.

'Garth, you can't just walk into my room. We had an agreement—'

'It's not me that's breaking it, Faye. You gave your word that there'd be no dates with Haines—'

'I didn't make a date with him—'

'*Don't lie to me!* You were with him tonight. I saw you as I drove home.'

'I said I didn't make a date with him, not that I didn't see him. I bumped into Kendall as I came out of the concert and had a drink with him. That's all.'

'Not quite all. You were kissing him.'

'You really studied us, didn't you? Or are you just protecting your investment?'

'I don't like people who don't keep their word.'

'It was an accident.'

'Was kissing him an accident?'

'No, I did that because I wanted to,' she said defiantly.

'And to hell with me?'

'I never gave you a thought,' she said, meeting his eyes. 'What's this all about, Garth? You said yourself there's nothing for us now but to see this through to the end and say goodbye.'

'Perhaps I've changed my mind,' he said, reaching for her determinedly.

'Oh, no!' She put up a hand. 'Our agreement—'

'You broke it, Faye. Now it's my turn. I don't like being overlooked and I'm not going to be any longer.' Before she could protest he covered her mouth with his own, kissing her with fierce, angry intent.

As soon as their lips touched Faye knew what had been missing from Kendall's kiss. The opposition of her mind meant nothing while Garth could still cause vibrations of pleasure to go through her at his lightest touch. Anger at the way he simply took what he wanted warred with a pleasure that her body had once known, and for which it still yearned.

She couldn't cope with her feelings because they reminded her how totally he could possess her. Worse still, they brought back the hot, sweet nights of their early love. With that love gone, it was cruel that her flesh still responded to him.

'Let me go, Garth,' she told him, eyes blazing.

'Why should I? This was what you wanted the other night.'

'Like you, I've changed my mind. Let me go now.'

'Am I trespassing on Kendall Haines's property? Do you think I care?'

'I'm not his property, and I'm not yours.'

'You were mine once, because that was how you wanted it. You gave yourself to me completely, with trust and love. Do you remember that, Faye?'

'Don't,' she whispered.

'Why not? Do you think I'm going to let you wipe our past away as though it never existed? It did exist. It *lived*, and it's part of us both, however much you wish it wasn't.'

She struggled to speak firmly. She wouldn't let him win. 'I don't remember anything, Garth. The past is dead.'

'Damn you,' he said softly.

He took possession of her mouth, and the pleasure was so poignant that she gasped. The hand she put up was meant to push him away but somehow it ended by caressing him instead, fingers in his hair, turning and twisting, enjoying the springy feel.

He tugged at the belt of her bathrobe until it came loose and he could pull the robe from her shoulders and embrace her totally. Half knowing what she did, Faye began to open the buttons of his shirt. She wanted everything about him: his agility and strength, his skill and tenderness, all the things that had once been hers. So much had gone for ever but there was still the pleasure of clinging to him, feeling his hands wandering over her, making her come alive.

Garth held her against him, looking down into her flushed, dreamy face.

'You remember,' he said arrogantly. 'You pretend not to, but you do. You remember everything, how much I want you, how much you want me—'

'It's not true,' she gasped.

'I can make it true. I'm still there, aren't I, Faye? Deny it as much as you like, *I'm still there.*'

'Yes,' she said in a helpless whisper. 'But, Garth, please—this isn't the answer.'

'What is the answer?' he demanded between kisses. 'Cosy little chats to relive every detail of our mistakes? Who needs words when we can talk like this?'

He smothered her mouth with his own, silencing all further argument. Faye could feel the last of her reason slipping away in the tide of passion that flowed over her.

She felt the silk of the counterpane beneath her back, the slight sinking of the mattress as Garth lay down beside her. His eyes seemed to feast on her, like a starving man presented with a banquet, and he ran a hand appreciatively over her slim frame.

'You managed the other seven pounds, I see,' he murmured admiringly. 'I had a feeling you'd do what you set your mind to. Looks great.'

He didn't wait for her to speak, but kissed her again. Longing flooded her. It was useless to protest to herself. She wanted Garth as much as he wanted her, and now she could only yield with a deep sigh of fulfilment.

He groaned as he pulled her against him, enfolding her in his arms and running his hands over her beautiful form. Their hearts and minds might have parted, but on this level nothing had changed. Ten years ago their physical harmony had been immediate and ecstatic. It was the same now. He knew how to please her, and he used his knowledge to the full.

Although it was their physical need that drove them, he was still the considerate lover that she remembered. He knew how to wait, to give her time to feel easy with him again. Looking up, she met his eyes and found them brooding over her like a miser with recovered treasure.

'You're still mine,' he murmured. 'You always were mine, and you always will be.'

She knew she should dispute this, but the delight flooding through her left no room for argument. Whatever the future held, she was his at this moment and her heart knew it.

The time they'd spent apart had brought its changes and as lovers they were strangers again. But they'd been strangers the first time they made love and it had been wonderful. Now Faye felt almost as she had then, breathless with eagerness, not sure what to expect of him but hoping for everything.

She thought she surprised a moment of hesitancy in his face, as though he, too, were moving cautiously as he reclaimed unfamiliar ground. She knew that look. It meant he wanted to be reassured. So she did so, touching his face gently, one of their old signals, and the result was all she'd hoped. His embrace grew stronger, more confident and possessive. Just as it had been that first time.

And something else was the same, the beauty and wonder of becoming one with him. Once she'd been sure that life could hold no more happiness than this. Now she knew for certain that it was true. The years without him had been a lonely ache of desolation, and secretly she'd always been waiting to come home.

There was a new edge to their passion. Now she, too,

had confidence. She knew herself as a woman who could drive this attractive man wild. What was happening had always been bound to happen.

She murmured his name and he looked at her quickly. 'Faye?' he said. 'Faye?' It was a question, as though he thought she might vanish from his arms.

She held him close, demanding more and more, and he gave freely and bountifully. Their climax was a burst of dazzling light, a flowering of the world that left her exhausted, trembling and utterly satiated.

She could see that it was the same with him. He was gasping slightly from the lengths to which she'd driven him and his face registered pure amazement. Faye wondered if her own face revealed her feeling of triumph.

She looked at him out of eyes that were hazy with fulfilment. Her whole body was relaxed as it hadn't been for two years. The world was a good place after all.

'I didn't mean that to happen,' he said slowly, watching her.

'Didn't you?' she asked softly. 'I thought you'd meant it to happen from the start.'

'I made you a promise—'

Oh, yes, she thought vaguely. The promise.

'It's too late to worry about that,' she murmured, wondering why he was making a fuss about it. Unconsciously, her lips curved into a blissful smile.

'Don't smile at me like that,' he said hoarsely. 'Not unless you want to drive me mad. *Faye!*'

He took hold of her shoulders to give her a little shake, but he didn't let go. He couldn't. The moment he touched her they both knew their desire was far from exhausted. And this time it was even more irresistible, because of what they'd both discovered.

He said her name once more, before his lips descended on her mouth. Faye gave a sigh of anticipation, and it all began again.

Garth was already downstairs when Faye descended next morning. She waited for him to look up, for the consciousness that would be between them. Perhaps he would smile.

But there was only trouble in his eyes when he raised his head. 'I owe you an apology,' he said in a low voice.

'An—?'

'Look, I know what you're going to say. I broke my word. You told me to stay away from you or the deal would be off. Please—' He raised his hand when she tried to speak.

Faye's voice faded at once. She couldn't have forced the words out through the stone that was encasing her heart.

'Just hear me out,' Garth insisted. 'I swear that nothing like it will ever happen again. I was in a bad state last night, business worries, nothing serious, but I wasn't myself. I'm sure you're angry, Faye, but there's no need to be. It's over, finished. I'll draw a line under it, if you will.'

'By all means, let's draw a line under it,' she said. 'Nothing could suit me better.'

CHAPTER NINE

AT LAST it was time for the children to return from Cornwall. After that first delight, Faye was relieved to have their laughter filling the house. The cheerful sound covered the spaces between herself and Garth.

Their passionate lovemaking, so intense and shattering at the time, seemed to have slipped past without leaving any impression on him. Instead of growing closer to her, he'd seemed determined to keep his distance.

The morning afterwards he had been able to speak only of his broken promise. But he'd mentioned that while they had lain together and she'd put his mind at rest. She couldn't recall her own words exactly, but she knew she'd said that she wasn't angry about the promise. His obsession with it next day had made no sense, unless he had been using it as an excuse.

As the days went by she realized that this was the answer. There was a constraint in Garth's manner that hadn't been there before, and he was seldom at home. When they spoke it was usually to discuss the anniversary celebrations that were nearly on them.

One evening he said, 'I'm going to Newcastle tomorrow and I have to leave at seven in the morning. There's no need for you to get up then.'

'All right,' she said quietly. It was obvious that he didn't want her. 'How long will you be away?'

'I might stay overnight. Word's already getting around about the Diamond Range and I'm meeting a consortium that may put in a big order. It'll be a great coup if I bring it off before the range is even launched.'

'That's wonderful,' she said politely. 'Will you be going in the plane?'

'No, someone's driving me up. I can make calls in the back of the car without being disturbed.'

She was awake before Garth left next morning and lay listening to him moving about downstairs, until the front door closed and she heard him drive away.

Sunk in her own thoughts she barely heard the children chattering over breakfast, but at last the word 'zoo' reached her.

'What, darling?' she asked Cindy.

'Daddy said he's taking us to the zoo on Saturday. He will be back by then, won't he, Mummy?'

'I'm sure he will, pet. He's due back tomorrow.'

But she wondered if Garth had remembered the zoo. He'd mentioned staying over for one night, but that might stretch to a second. It would be wise to send him a reminder. Mary, his secretary, would be in Newcastle with him, but she had an office junior whom Faye could telephone.

But when she called his headquarters, she found herself talking to Mary herself. She was friendly, and one of the few people in the office whom Faye found congenial.

'I thought you'd have gone away with Garth,' Faye said.

'I was supposed to but I've got family problems at the moment,' Mary told her. 'I'd rather not be away overnight. Luckily Lysandra came to my rescue.'

'You mean—Lysandra has gone with him?'

'Yes, wasn't that kind of her?'

'Very kind,' Faye murmured.

She gave her message, which Mary promised to deliver, and hung up, trying to silence the disquiet in her breast. She'd settled with herself that she wasn't jealous of Lysandra, so what did it matter? After the divorce, Garth could marry anyone he liked.

'Oh, no, he can't!' she said suddenly, aloud. 'I'm not having that woman become stepmother to my children.'

It was a relief to know the reason for her disturbance.

It was good to have the children home and she was determined to make the most of their company. A shopping trip in town turned into a spending spree and they returned with new trainers and sweaters with zoo animals printed on them. They immediately put them on and headed for the garden.

'Hey, save those sweaters for the zoo,' Faye called. 'You'll get them dirty out there.'

'We won't, Mummy, honestly,' Adrian called, but even as he spoke he was tussling with Barker for the ball. He finally got it out of the dog's mouth, and rubbed his hand over the elephant's head on his chest.

'Never mind,' Faye grinned. 'I can always wash them before Saturday.'

Barker was like a child himself, bouncing and rolling about, chasing after every ball and uttering deafening barks of delight. The trust and understanding between the three of them was lovely to see.

'Tea in fifteen minutes,' Faye called, and went into the kitchen. She reached up for Barker's dry biscuits, for she knew he couldn't bear to be left out of a meal. He was especially fond of the red ones, so she took two red ones apart. Always afterwards it was imprinted in her memory how she'd smiled as she'd set the biscuits by the kettle in the last split second before the world was turned upside down.

At first she hardly registered that Barker had suddenly made a different sound. But then it was followed by a dreadful scream from Cindy and the little girl came flying into the kitchen.

'Mummy, Mummy! *Come quickly!*'

Barker was lying on his side, heaving, his eyes full of pain. 'He was running and he just stopped and fell over,' Adrian cried.

'I'll call the vet,' Faye said urgently and raced back to the house. Adrian came with her but Cindy stayed with Barker, holding his head in her arms and murmuring comfort.

'They're sending an ambulance for him,' she told Adrian. 'It'll be here any moment. They'll make him better.'

She tried to sound convinced, but she knew what had happened, and how it would probably end. But she would protect her children until the last moment.

Then Adrian said, 'Someone at school saw his grandfather have a heart attack and he told us what happened.'

Their eyes met and she saw how grown up her son was. 'Yes,' she said. 'I think Barker's had a heart attack. He's quite old.'

Adrian's eyes were wet and he closed them for a moment while his hand groped for Faye's. When he opened them he said, 'We mustn't tell Cindy yet. She's just a child.'

'The vet's very good,' Faye said. 'Barker might come through it.'

The ambulance arrived and two attendants moved the dog gently onto a stretcher. Cindy walked beside him, stroking his head and fighting back her tears in case he should see them and be dismayed. She never doubted that he understood human reactions.

'I'm going with him,' she said, preparing to climb into the ambulance.

'No, darling, they've got things to do for him in there,' Faye said. 'We'll follow right behind in the car.'

On the journey Cindy's tears flowed unrestrained. Faye saw Adrian put his arms around her. His own face was pale and set.

'You did this!' Faye said to Garth in her mind. 'You broke their hearts and I'll never forgive you for it.'

At the hospital the intensive care room was all ready for them. Miss McGeorge examined Barker carefully, listening to his chest, pulling back the lids of his eyes, which had closed.

'X-ray his chest,' she told Andy, her assistant. 'As soon as that's done give him an injection of painkiller, and put him on a drip.'

'Is he going to be all right?' Adrian asked tensely.

Miss McGeorge hesitated. 'He's old,' she said, 'and I think it's bad. We'll do our best, but...'

It seemed an age while they waited for the results of Barker's X-rays. The children were unusually quiet, but their tight grip on their mother's hand revealed their distress and their need of her.

At last Miss McGeorge emerged and her heavy face told the whole story. 'I'm afraid it was a massive heart attack,' she said. 'There's really no chance for him. It might be kinder to put him to sleep now.'

'No!' Cindy's cry of agony was like a sword cutting through the words. 'He's got to stay alive. *He's got to.*'

'Darling—' Faye put her arms about the child '—he's suffering now—'

'But he wouldn't if they made him well,' she sobbed. 'I love him, Mummy. He can't die, not if I love him. Make them save him.'

'I don't know how,' she said helplessly.

'But Daddy will.' The tears were still rolling down Cindy's face, but suddenly it was illuminated by hope. 'Daddy will know what to do, because he gave me Barker. Please, Mummy, call him.'

'Cindy—' Adrian put his arms protectively around his sister '—Daddy isn't a vet. He can't make Barker well.'

'He can!' Cindy shouted. 'Daddy can do anything in the whole world. He can, he *can!*'

'Try to keep Barker alive,' Faye told Miss McGeorge. She pulled out her mobile and dialled Garth's mobile. But it had been switched off. Desperately she dialled the office where he'd said he would be. The operator put her through to Lysandra.

'I need to speak to my husband urgently.'

'I'm afraid Mr Clayton is out at the moment.' Lysandra's tone was sweet with satisfaction at being able to refuse Faye.

'Please ask him to call me on my mobile the moment he returns. Tell him we're all at the vet; Barker is very ill and Cindy is relying on him.'

She stressed the urgency again and hung up. 'Daddy's going to call back soon,' she promised.

An hour passed. Still the phone didn't ring.

'He's not going to call, is he?' Adrian asked in a toneless voice.

'He is,' Cindy told him fiercely. 'He's going to call any moment now.'

'He might not have come back yet,' Faye said. Inwardly she was filled with dread. Garth had been elated at the thought of pulling off this coup. To get it, he would do anything. But would that mean reverting to his old ways, and putting his daughter last?

'There's a drinks machine just down the corridor,' she said. 'I'm going to get us something.'

When Faye had gone, Cindy's attention became riveted on the bag she'd left on the floor. Adrian frowned as he saw his sister reach inside and pull out the mobile phone.

'What are you doing?' he asked.

'I'm going to call Daddy.'

'But you don't know his number.'

'It was the last thing Mummy dialled,' Cindy said, triumphantly pressing the redial button.

While Adrian regarded her with a kind of awe, she listened to the ringing tone from the other end.

'Blow your nose,' Adrian advised, holding out his own, clean handkerchief. 'You don't want them to think you're just a little kid.'

She gave him a look of gratitude and did so, just before someone answered.

'My name is Cindy Clayton,' she said with dignity. 'And I want to talk to Daddy.'

'Just one moment.' The operator sounded confused.

A moment later Cindy heard another voice on the line. It was softly implacable and she hated it on instinct. 'I'm afraid Mr Clayton is too busy to talk now.'

'But it's Cindy. I know he'll talk to me.'

'I'm sorry, he has some very important men to see. I've given him your message and he says he's sure you'll understand why he can't talk to you now.'

Cindy began to tremble. 'But it's Barker,' she said in a stammering voice.

'I'm sure it is, and he'll call you just as soon as he's free. But he really can't spare the time just now.'

Faye returned from the machine with her hands full to find Cindy staring ahead, her face a ghastly colour.

'It's Daddy,' Adrian said in a hard voice. 'She called him. He wouldn't even talk to her.'

Cindy's tears had dried now. The father in whom she'd pinned her faith had simply brushed her aside. There were no tears for such a devastating betrayal. Only silent despair.

'He said—' she choked at last '—that—he was sure— I'd understand wh-why he couldn't talk to me.'

'Oh, did he?' Faye said ominously. 'Well, I *don't* understand and I'm going to tell him so.'

She called again, hoping against hope that she might be answered by someone other than Lysandra. But the fates were against her.

'I wish to be put through to my husband, *at once*,' she said firmly.

Lysandra's voice was equally firm. 'I'm very sorry, but Mr Clayton's orders were explicit. He's engaged in serious negotiations and must not be disturbed.'

'Tell him it's an emergency and I *have* to speak to him. Do it right now.'

'Mrs Clayton, I'm sorry but you force me to be blunt. I take my orders from Garth, not from you.' The phone went dead.

The children were watching her anxiously, but their faces had changed. Instead of the blind trust that had been there only a short time ago, now they looked ready to endure even more disappointment. How much more of this could they take? she wondered.

'All right,' she said with sudden determination. 'Time to take the gloves off.'

They watched her, puzzled, as she called Mary. 'I need to get to Newcastle as fast as possible, and that means by plane. How can I reach Garth's pilot?'

She heard the little gasp before Mary assumed her

well-trained voice. 'Bill should be at home. Garth gave him a few days off.'

'I'd like his number, please.'

'You're going to ask him to fly you there? But Bill only takes orders from Garth himself. Wouldn't it be better if I called Garth—?'

'Fine! If you can get through to him, get him to call me,' Faye said, suddenly hopeful.

But in two minutes Mary was back on the line, seething.

'That woman,' she said in tones of deep loathing. 'She said she'd get him to call me back, ''when he could spare a moment''. Garth's never refused to talk to me before. OK. Here's Bill's mobile number. And good luck.'

'Thanks. I'm going to need it.'

Bill was a good natured, lazy young man who preferred sleeping to any other activity except flying. Faye roused him from a nap, but when he heard what she wanted he was fully alert.

'I can't take the plane out unless Garth orders me,' he said aghast.

Faye took a deep breath and crossed her fingers before saying, 'But he has ordered you. I'm acting with his blessing. He wants you to fly me there at once. I can't tell you details, but it's a real emergency. Believe me, if Garth misses out on this, and then finds it was because you disobeyed his orders to help me, well—I just don't know what he'll do.'

It was barefaced blackmail, the sort of action that once she would never have dared, and her heart was beating hard at her own temerity. But all that mattered now was that Garth should put Cindy and Adrian first. If he couldn't save Barker, at least he could save his children's faith in him.

Bill was nervous. 'Couldn't you get Garth to confirm—?'

'No, I couldn't,' she said firmly. 'This is a matter of life and death and I've no time to waste.'

'All right, Mrs Clayton, but you won't mind if I call him first—'

'You won't get through. He's not talking to anyone. Besides,' she added with a casualness she was far from feeling, 'I just wish I could be a fly on the wall if you manage to haul him out of a big meeting to ask him if his wife's a liar.' She even managed a laugh. 'Still, it's your head on the block.'

'Yes, it is,' he said thoughtfully. 'Oh, well, I suppose if you tell me it's all right—'

'I do. The responsibility is all mine. I'll be there in half an hour. Please have the engine running.' She hung up and leaned against the wall, drained and shaking from tension. That had been *her* speaking, gauche, shy Faye who'd once looked out at the world from under Garth's shadow. Now that seemed a very long time ago.

A suggestion that the children should go home was instantly vetoed. Neither of them would leave their friend. Faye called Nancy and told her to come to the surgery.

'It's not Daddy's fault,' she told the children. 'There's been a misunderstanding and I'm going up there to sort it out.'

She only wished she felt as confident as she sounded.

She left the moment Nancy arrived and began the drive to the airport. Her stomach was churning with nerves. She had no idea what was waiting for her in Newcastle. Garth had tried to block out his family again, and when she gatecrashed his meeting he would be furious. If only she didn't fail! If only she could keep her nerve long enough to confront him!

An efficient machine took over as soon as she arrived. Someone took her car to park it. Someone else told her Bill was ready to leave at once. The engine was running just as she'd said, and in a few minutes they were airborne.

'There'll be a car waiting the moment we land,' Bill said.

'Thank you, Bill. You're very efficient.'

'That's what Mr Clayton says,' Bill said gloomily. 'What he'll say to me after today I don't like to think.'

'But I told you this was with his blessing.'

'That's right, you did,' he said in a voice of deep gloom.

'You just stick to it that you believed me. I'll take the flak.'

As he'd promised, the car was there and in a few moments she was delivered at the headquarters of Garth's clients. A man on the front desk politely enquired her business.

'I have to see Mr Clayton. I'm his wife, and it's extremely urgent.'

The confident way she spoke had its effect. The man showed her the lift and said, 'Top floor, madam.'

One hurdle over.

On the top floor there was a young woman at a reception desk who rose and tried to block her way.

'I'm sorry, but my instructions are to let nobody through,' she said, smiling but implacable.

Faye also smiled. 'If you don't let me through I shall scream the place down,' she said.

'Then I should have to call Security,' the receptionist said.

'Do so,' Faye said almost amiably. She felt cool and in control. To call anyone, the receptionist would have to move out of her way.

Too late the young woman realized this and for a split second she hesitated between the desk and Faye. That instant was enough. Faye moved her aside and swept on. Over her shoulder she could hear the receptionist telephoning someone and hurried lest security guards should appear.

But it was Lysandra who came out and stood in her path. She was holding a file across her chest, as though in defence, and she looked very much in command. But then Faye's heightened senses made her acutely aware of the other woman's pallor and unease. Suddenly Lysandra wasn't confident any more. Her knuckles were white where they grasped the file and she was angry and afraid.

'Let me pass,' Faye told her quietly.

'Absolutely not! Garth says he doesn't want to be bothered by disturbances now—'

'Well he's going to be whether he wants to or not. Now, I'll tell you for the last time, *get out of my way.*'

Lysandra seemed to take root in the ground and for a moment Faye's new-found courage almost failed. Then she remembered Cindy's frantic sobs and Adrian's white-faced tension and knew that nothing was going to stop her.

Moving so fast that she almost couldn't follow it herself, she seized the file Lysandra was holding and sent it whirling across the floor. Lysandra gasped with outrage, made a small lunge then thought better of it. But it was too late. Faye took hold of her shoulders, swung her around and marched on.

A set of double doors loomed before her. Faye took a deep breath and was through them before she had time to think. She found herself in a large room, dominated by a long table, around which sat a dozen men. At the far end, deep in paperwork, sat Garth, so engrossed that he knew nothing until a silence fell. The other men stared, nonplussed, as the pale, distraught-looking woman strode into the room and walked to the head of the table.

At last Garth looked up, astonishment on his face as he saw his wife. 'Faye? What are you doing here?'

'Are you really surprised to see me, after the message you sent?'

'What message?'

'Don't pretend not to know what I mean,' she said angrily. 'I came to talk to you, and that's what I'm going to do.'

'Then we'll go next door,' he said calmly. 'Excuse me a moment, gentlemen.'

He took her arm and drew her through a side door into a little room. When they were alone his urbane manner fell away and she could see that he was coldly angry.

'Now, perhaps you'll tell me what you mean by bursting in and speaking to me like that in front of my colleagues,' he said in a tight voice.

'I wouldn't have needed to if you'd deigned to speak to me on the phone,' Faye said fiercely. 'Why don't *you* tell me what you mean by sending your daughter a message by Lysandra Bates that you were too busy to talk to her.'

'What the devil are you talking about?'

'Oh, please, Garth! Don't pretend ignorance. It's all

been an act, hasn't it? Letting Cindy think she meant something to you, then brushing her aside when she needs you most. You've broken her heart, but why should you care as long as business isn't disturbed?'

'What do you mean?' he interrupted. 'Why does she need me? What's happened?'

'Barker's had a massive heart attack. He's dying!'

He closed his eyes. 'Oh, dear God! No!'

'I told you he was very ill when I called.'

'When did you call? This is the first I've heard of it. Who did you speak to?'

'Lysandra. She said you were out and I left a message for you, saying Barker was ill and please call me back urgently, but you never did. So Cindy called, and that woman said she was sure Cindy'd understand why you couldn't talk to her. But she *doesn't*. She was sure you could cure him. She thought you could do anything in the world—always assuming she can get in touch to ask you.'

'Faye, I'm telling you I knew nothing of this. Lysandra never passed any message on to me and I'm damned well going to find out why.'

He wrenched open the door. Lysandra was just outside, a nervous smile on her face. Now Faye understood why the other woman had been so alarmed at her appearance.

'What's this about a message from my wife that never reached me?' Garth demanded.

'I knew you didn't want to be interrupted,' Lysandra said smoothly.

'I never gave you authority to block out my wife,' he snapped.

'I'm sorry if I misunderstood your instructions, Mr Clayton. I thought I was acting for the best.'

'Were you acting for the best when you told Cindy that her father wouldn't speak to her?' Faye demanded. 'That wasn't a misunderstanding. It was a lie.'

'I agree,' Garth said, regarding Lysandra coldly. 'I gather that my eight-year-old daughter telephoned, herself, and you actually refused to put her on to me. How *dared* you do such a thing?'

Under the black look he was giving her, even the super-cool Lysandra quailed.

'I'm—I'm sorry,' she stammered. 'I assure you such a thing will never happen again.'

'It certainly won't, because you don't work for me any more,' Garth said flatly. 'Don't even set foot in the office again. I'll have your things sent on to you.'

Lysandra gasped. 'Garth—you can't mean that.'

'I can and I do. Get out of my sight.'

She placed a hand on his arm. 'Please, can we discuss this—alone?' She glanced significantly at Faye.

He shook her off. 'We have nothing to discuss alone. We never did, but I couldn't make you realize that. You were efficient at your job. That was my sole interest in you.'

Lysandra's face became distorted. 'You'll regret this,' she spat. 'How are you going to manage that meeting in there without my support?'

Garth eyed her narrowly. 'Don't ever fool yourself that I can't do without you, Lysandra. *Nobody* is indispensable to me. Anyway, that meeting is closing down because I'm leaving.'

'You can't,' Lysandra gasped. 'They'll never give you the contract—'

'Then they can give it to someone else. Now get out of my sight. I don't want to see you again.'

The look Lysandra gave Faye might have struck her

down if she hadn't had more important things to think of. As it was, she barely noticed.

'I'll send for the car,' Garth said when Lysandra had gone, 'and we'll drive back together.'

'No need. I came in your plane.'

'You—?' He stared at her for a moment, then seemed to pull himself together. 'Wait here.'

He marched back into the conference room and she could hear him explaining that a family tragedy had unfortunately made it necessary for him to leave.

A male voice expressed polite sympathy, but then said, 'You know we're behind schedule already. I hope we can continue this discussion tomorrow.'

'My time will be taken up for a week at the very least,' Garth replied. 'It might even be longer.'

There was a murmur. When the voice spoke again it had a slight edge. 'It must be a very close relative.'

'My daughter's dog is ill,' Garth said flatly and the murmur became a hum of disapproval.

'A dog? We're expected to put our plans on hold for a dog?'

'Not at all, gentlemen. I'll understand if you want to find another firm. I apologize for having wasted your time.'

Next moment he appeared in the side room where Faye was waiting, and said, 'Come on.' He took her arm and they went out to the lift together.

As they drove to the airport, Garth called Bill's mobile and spoke for a few minutes. When he hung up he was frowning. 'He's there at Newcastle Airport, waiting for us,' he said. 'You really did take the plane.'

'You thought I was making it up?'

'No, but—Bill answers only to me. How did you get him to do it?'

'I told him I had your authority.'

'You did *what*?'

'It was the only way.'

'And no doubt you also persuaded him not to call me and check?'

'Of course. I told him I'd like to be a fly on the wall when he asked you if your wife was a liar.'

Garth stared at her, something like fascination in his eyes. '*You* did *that*?'

'I had to. Don't get mad with Bill. It wasn't his fault.'

'I'm only too aware of that. I'm not mad, I'm just astounded at you doing all this. It's the sort of thing I'd have done, but—you?'

'Maybe we're more alike than you know.'

'I'm beginning to think we are.' He was still regarding her as if he were seeing her for the first time.

CHAPTER TEN

WHEN they reached the airport Bill was waiting apprehensively, but Garth eased his fears by remarking, 'Thanks for getting her here, Bill. Good work.'

On the flight home Faye told him all the details of Barker's attack. 'The vet says that at his age he hasn't much chance,' she said, and Garth groaned.

'Don't rub it in,' he said morosely.

'I'm not. I was just trying to make you see what a job you've got. Cindy's sure you can solve the problem.'

'I can certainly get the best specialist there is,' he said, becoming the Garth she knew.

His arrival at the animal hospital was greeted by a frenzy of delight and relief. 'I knew you'd come, I knew it,' Cindy squealed. 'Now Barker will be all right.'

'I'll do my best, darling,' he promised her, concealing his apprehension.

He tried to talk to Miss McGeorge in private, but the children refused to be excluded and the whole family gathered in the room where Barker was lying.

The vet laid it on the line. 'He's still alive,' she said, 'but there's no strength left in his heart. He'll have another attack in days. I ought to put him to sleep now.'

'No,' Garth said at once. 'There must be something that we can do. What about when people have heart attacks? You don't put them to sleep, do you? You give them operations to save them.'

'If you're talking about a bypass operation, there's only one man I know of who could tackle this.'

'Then get him.'

'He's abroad and not due back for days,' Miss McGeorge explained. 'It would cost you a fortune—'

'Do you think that matters?'

'And it isn't worth it. The animal is half dead now.'

'He's not "the animal", he's Barker,' Garth said firmly. 'And anything is worth it if it gives him a chance. What is this man's name?'

'James Wakeham.'

'Can you call him right now?'

Miss McGeorge sighed. 'Very well, I'll try.'

'Tell him he can have anything.'

James Wakeham was attending a conference in Belgium and it took a few nail-biting minutes to locate him. Cindy stayed by Barker, stroking his inert head and whispering words of love into his floppy ears.

At last Wakeham was located. Miss McGeorge explained the situation and then went into a detailed clinical description of Barker's state.

'Yes, I see,' she said at last. 'No, of course not Well, that's what I said— I'll explain—I'm sure they'll understand. Hey!' She spluttered indignantly as Garth removed the phone from her hand.

'Mr Wakeham, I'm Garth Clayton, and Barker is my children's dog. I want him kept alive at all costs, and I'm told you're the only person who can do it.'

The voice that reached him was thin and cool. 'I understand that, of course, but from what I hear of his description there would be no point in attempting an operation.'

'You don't know there's no point if you don't try it,' Garth protested desperately. 'When you get here you may find it looks more hopeful. I'll pay all your expenses and any fee you like. Just name it.'

'Mr Clayton, I appreciate your feelings, but I have a meeting at any moment and I'm afraid I can't break into it for a hopeless case. Will you please put me back to Miss McGeorge?'

'No, I damned well won't,' Garth said furiously. 'Barker may be just a hopeless case to you, but to my children he's a friend that they love. What's so important about a damned meeting that you can't leave it for a sick dog?'

'I'm preparing a very important paper—'

'The paper can wait. My dog can't. You're his last chance.'

'Your dog has *no* chance. An operation would be a total waste of time and I don't have the time to waste.' The phone went dead.

It took a long time for Garth to replace the receiver, because he was trying to come to terms with the fact that his money and power, the talismans he relied on, were useless. He was almost in a state of shock.

The room seemed to have developed an echoing quality, and details stood out with alarming sharpness. Cindy had climbed onto a chair next to Barker and was lying against him, her arms as far around him as they would go, her face buried in his thick fur. She was sobbing frantically, having understood that her father had failed.

Adrian's face was pale and set, as though he were clenching his teeth. Faye was standing beside Cindy, stroking her head and murmuring useless words of comfort. She looked up and her expression was the hardest thing of all to bear. She hated him. She'd warned him of this on the day they'd found Barker and he'd brushed her aside for his own selfish convenience. Now his children were paying the price in anguish and Faye would never forgive him. Nor did he deserve to be forgiven.

The echo vanished as he controlled his shock. The room became normal again. But his daughter was still crying her heart out and something agonizing was happening to his own heart, as if it were being torn out of him.

'What did he say?' Miss McGeorge asked.

'He won't come,' Garth said bleakly. 'It's more important to go to some meeting.'

'Mr Wakeham is a brilliant surgeon, but I'm afraid he's ruled by vanity. He wouldn't take on a case as far advanced as this. A failure would spoil his record.'

Faye stepped back as Garth approached Cindy and touched her head. 'Darling,' he said tentatively.

She looked up at him with a flash of hope that he might have thought of something at the last minute.

'I'm sorry,' he said heavily. 'There's nothing I can do.'

'There *is*,' she insisted. 'There must be. You can't just give up.'

'That man was our last chance and he won't come.'

'But you could *make* him come.'

'I can't force him.'

'You could if you really wanted to.'

'Cindy, I do really want to—'

'No, you don't. You don't care if Barker dies.' She was heaving with sobs as she fought to get the words out. 'I thought—when—you came—everything would be all right—'cos you can do anything—but you don't want to—'

'Darling, please believe me—'

Garth reached for her but she fought off his embrace wildly, screaming, 'You don't! You don't care! You don't care about anyone! I hate you, *I hate you, I HATE*

YOU!' She flung herself into Faye's arms, sobbing violently.

Garth backed out of the room, his horrified eyes fixed on his daughter.

By now it was late. The animal hospital had spacious grounds. Garth didn't know how long he walked through them, pursued by his own thoughts like avenging furies.

This was the day Faye had warned him would come; the day when his sins would come home to him. And they were terrible sins. Wandering wretchedly under the trees, Garth accused himself of the worst kind of selfishness, neglecting his little daughter then using her love to get his own way.

He remembered her joy when he'd appeared at Faye's house. It was completely irrational that she should have still loved him when he'd given her so little. He knew he deserved no praise for having kept her love. It was to the child's credit, not his own. Uncritical devotion was a part of Cindy's character, as it was with her mother. With both of them he'd taken it as a right. And he'd betrayed both of them.

His only saving grace was that Cindy's adoration had touched his heart and he'd opened his arms to her with true warmth. Now their mutual love was genuine. But that was no credit to him either, for who could help loving Cindy?

And there was Adrian, who'd been rightly suspicious of his father at first. He'd regarded that as a challenge and set out to overcome it. With the Outland incident he hadn't even seen the pit that yawned at his feet. But for Faye, he would have fallen in. He'd meant to use what Adrian had told him, but in the very act of signing the documents something had held him back. He'd torn them up and even tossed away the pen, as though it was contaminated. He'd lost the land, but he'd gained his son. Thanks to Faye's timely warning.

In the darkness he experienced the most terrible depths of self-disgust. His beloved children were enduring heartbreak and it was his fault. His wife had abandoned him as a lost cause and he knew now that she'd been right. He blighted everything he touched and nothing could live near him. Cindy's hate was a dreadful punishment, but infinitely worse was the knowledge that he deserved it.

He sat down on a bench and buried his head in his hands. He'd always been the man in control, but now that it mattered as never before he was totally helpless.

He felt a light touch on his head, and looked up to find his daughter regarding him. He almost flinched away from her, but there was no judgement in her small, tear-stained face.

'I'm sorry, darling,' he said huskily. 'I did my best. Truly I did. But I don't know what else to do...'

'It's not your fault, Daddy,' she said gently. 'I'm sorry for what I said.'

Her generosity brought tears to his eyes. For a moment he couldn't speak. When he tried to say something the words came out haltingly.

'It *is* my fault— He was always too old— I should have insisted on another dog—'

She shook her head decidedly. 'Then it wouldn't have been Barker.'

'But you'd have had him for a lot longer—'

'It wouldn't have been the same,' Cindy said simply. 'Barker is—*Barker*. Even if we didn't have him for long, we did have him.'

'A few short weeks,' he murmured, unwilling to let himself off the hook.

'But we had those weeks, that's what counts.'

There was an ache in his throat that made it hard to speak. 'I wanted—to save him for you, darling, but—but—'

Overwhelmed, he put his arms about her and held her close, his shoulders shaking. She hugged him back. 'It's all right, Daddy,' she whispered. 'Truly, it's all right.'

He looked up at her, and she stroked his face in wonder. 'Are you crying?'

'No, of course not,' he said hastily. 'Daddies don't cry.'

'Don't they really? Mummies do.'

He tensed. 'Does your mother cry?'

'She cried a lot when we went away two years ago. I didn't understand. Why did she leave you if it made her so unhappy?'

'Perhaps it made her even more unhappy to stay,' he said slowly. 'Does she cry now?'

'I don't know. Sometimes I think, but she doesn't let on.'

They held each other in silence. Several times he thought she was about to speak, but she always hesitated. 'Daddy,' she said at last.

'Yes, darling?'

'I think—we ought to—stop trying to keep Barker alive.'

He looked closely into her face. 'Do you really mean that?'

'It's not kind to let him suffer.' Suddenly the tears were pouring down her cheeks. 'Oh, Daddy, I love him so much—but if you love someone—you've got to let them go—if it's best for them.' She clung to him, not sobbing as before, but weeping softly with resignation.

'Cindy, are you sure you mean that?'

'Yes, yes—*I mean it, I mean it—*'

Garth hugged her tightly, wondering at his child's courage, so much greater than his own. He saw his son standing quietly in the shadows. 'We should ask Adrian what he thinks,' he said, desperately playing for time.

Adrian was very pale. 'I've been listening. Cindy's right.'

Garth held out an arm and his son went into its circle. The three of them clung together. Faye, watching unobserved, silently backed away. Something painful was happening in her heart. Tonight Garth had become again the warm, emotional man she'd fallen in love with, and what she'd feared most had happened. Her feelings for him flowed freely again, and it hurt.

He joined her a few minutes later. His self reproach was painful to see. 'I'm useless,' he said desperately. 'There's not a thing I can do—not a thing—' His voice trailed away. He was staring into the middle distance.

'What is it?' Faye asked.

'I'd forgotten—' he said slowly. 'I should have remembered before— There *is* something I can do.' He began to walk urgently around the building to where the car was parked.

'Garth,' she said, following him. 'What is it?'

'I'd forgotten what he said—but it may not be too late. Tell Miss McGeorge to keep Barker alive tonight at all costs. And call Bill. Tell him to take off as soon as possible for Brussels Airport to collect James Wakeham.'

Faye heard the car door slam and the vehicle pull away fast.

*   *   *

The door was opened by a pretty young woman with long, auburn hair, no make-up and an intense expression.

'I'm looking for Kendall Haines,' Garth said, puzzled. 'Does he live here?'

'Yes, come in.' Garth gave her his name and she stood back and called into the house, 'There's a Mr Clayton for you, love.'

Kendall appeared. It seemed to Garth that he was smoothing down his hair, but he was too preoccupied with his errand to observe much. 'I have to talk to you urgently,' he said without preamble.

Kendall showed him into the front room and said, 'Coffee please, Jane.'

'Yes, Ken.' She spoke eagerly and rushed into the kitchen as if he'd offered her a treat.

'I need your help,' Garth said. 'My children's dog is dying. His one chance is an operation, but the best man for that is James Wakeham and he's abroad. He says it's not worth returning. But I remember your telling me that he's a friend of yours.'

'You've spoken to Wakeham?'

'Yes. I told him to name his own price, but I can't budge him. He kept talking about his conference, the important people he had to see. You're his friend. Can't you make him understand that none of those things matter if it means hurting a child?'

'We're not precisely friends,' Kendall said slowly.

'But he owes you a favour—'

'Possibly.' Kendall stood for a moment, sunk in thought.

'Haines, for God's sake!' Garth said desperately. 'If you want me to plead, I will. I'll do anything, but you must get that man back here, because otherwise—' he

paused and a shudder went through him '—otherwise
I've done something unforgivably selfish and cruel.'

'But even if I do convince him, he may not get a seat
on the plane at such short notice.'

'No problem. My own plane has already taken off to
collect him.'

'You're a man of great self-confidence, I see.'

'No,' Garth said heavily. 'None at all.'

'Do you have his number?' Garth gave it to him and
Kendall dialled. From the conversation that followed
Garth deduced that Wakeham wasn't immediately avail-
able, but would call back soon.

Jane entered with a tray of fresh coffee and poured
for them both. She handed Kendall his cup as he was
putting the phone down.

'Can I do anything else for you?' she asked eagerly.

'Yes, finish those papers we were working on in the
study.'

'Nothing here?' she asked, sounding disappointed.

'Just leave us alone, there's a dear,' Kendall said
kindly.

'If you want me, you'll be sure to call me?'

'I promise.'

'My secretary,' Kendall said when the door had closed
behind Jane. 'We were working late.'

'At this hour? She must be very obliging,' Garth said
with a slight edge on his voice.

'I know what you're getting at, but who's fault is it?
I was happy when Faye worked for me, but you wrecked
that. Jane's good at her job and she's always there when
I need her.'

'You mean, unlike Faye?'

'It was Faye's own choice to drift away. She returned
to you.'

A strange confusion of feelings warred within Garth. He should be glad that this man was getting out of his way, but his dominant feeling was one of anger. How dare this jerk dump Faye!

'I'd hardly say that she returned to me,' he said cautiously.

'But you're determined to get her back, aren't you? If you want to impress her, it was a shrewd move, coming here. Maybe that's why you came yourself instead of asking her to approach me.'

Garth stared, shocked into speechlessness. It simply hadn't occurred to him to send Faye.

The phone rang and Kendall answered. 'James,' he said heartily. 'Long time, no see. I'm here begging a favour—well, to call one in actually, since you still owe me for keeping quiet about that little matter— All right, you old dog, I was only joking. Actually, this is serious. You spoke to a friend of mine earlier— That's right, Garth Clayton—'

Garth had never doubted his own courage before, but suddenly he couldn't bear to listen. Everything in the world hung on this conversation. He left the room and stood in the hallway, nerves stretched to breaking point, until Kendall looked out.

'He's agreed,' he said, and Garth had to clutch the wall against the dizzying surge of relief. 'You'd better tell him about the plane yourself.'

The conversation was short and curt. Wakeham had been convinced, but was thoroughly displeased with everyone involved, himself included.

'I'll meet you this end,' Garth concluded.

When he'd hung up he allowed himself a few seconds' indulgence picturing Cindy's face when he told her. But it would take him fifteen minutes to get back to the surgery, and fifteen minutes could be a long time. He dialled at once and gave the news to Miss McGeorge, then to Faye.

'Tell the kids their old man pulled the rabbit out of the hat,' he said.

Her voice was husky. 'I knew you would. I just knew it.'

'Tell them quickly. Don't delay for a single moment. I'm on my way to the airport to fetch him.'

'Garth—'

'Yes?'

'Nothing. Just—take care.'

'I will. Tell Barker to hang in there.'

Kendall Haines was watching him with a calculating expression on his face. Garth tried to thank him, but Kendall shrugged him away.

'Before I go, there's one question I'd like to ask,' Garth said. 'Did you know that I owned Melkham Construction when you took my son on that demonstration?'

Kendall grinned. 'Of course I knew.'

'You were playing a damned devious game.'

'Don't give me moral outrage. You've played a few devious games in your time.'

'Not by making use of children.'

'All's fair in love and war,' Kendall said with a shrug.

'And you're in love with my wife?'

There was a small pause before Kendall said, 'I'm still engaged to her—as of now.'

'That's not an answer.'

'It's the only one you'll get.'

'Is she in love with you?'

'Ask her.'

'I have.'

'Then you already know the answer.'

In Kendall's position Garth knew he would demand to know what Faye had said. The other man's refusal to ask implied great self-restraint, or maybe something cooler. Garth recalled Jane and her worshipful expression. He saw Kendall looking at him wryly, bid him goodnight, and left quickly.

James Wakeham looked exactly as his voice had sounded, prissy and self-righteous. He gave Garth a nod to indicate that he forgave nothing, and got into the back seat of the car.

But his curtness fell away from him when he saw Barker and a cloak of authority descended like a mantle as he went through the readings on the machines.

'Stabilized? Good. Let's get to work then.'

The children were beyond words but their shining eyes, as they hugged their father, said everything. Cindy whispered, 'I knew you could do it.' She seemed convinced that Barker was certain to survive now and Garth lacked the heart to tell her any different.

Nancy, who'd gone home earlier, now reappeared with sandwiches and a flask of tea. Darkness had fallen, and the hospital was empty but for themselves and the two vets with Barker's life in their hands.

'The children ought to be home in bed,' Faye said ruefully. 'But I don't think they'll budge. Anyway, if Mr Wakeham can't save him, they'll want to be near Barker at the end.'

'Yes,' Garth said heavily. After his brief triumph it was salutary to be reminded that he might have achieved nothing at all.

'How did you get him to come over, after he refused?' Faye asked.

'Oh—I manoeuvred a bit.' He couldn't bring himself to tell her everything, in case it might seem like asking for praise.

'You mean you offered him more money?'

'Money!' he growled.

'Garth, I'm not criticizing, honestly. You were right to do anything that worked.'

Anything that worked. His own philosophy of life, but he'd meant money and power. It occurred to him that he'd always been thinking about these things. But this time it had been about something genuine and true. How strange, then, that he couldn't bring himself to speak of it!

Cindy and Adrian came and hugged him.

'Thanks, Dad,' Adrian said gruffly.

'Thank you, Daddy,' Cindy whispered.

'We're not out of the woods yet,' he warned them.

'But you did it,' Cindy insisted. 'You can do anything.'

He kissed her, but didn't say any more. Only he and his enemy knew the real sacrifice he'd made.

CHAPTER ELEVEN

THE operation lasted two hours.

'I did my best, but I can't work miracles,' James Wakeham said, emerging from the theatre and speaking brusquely. 'He's still alive, but it's too soon to be hopeful. You'll know by the morning.'

He resisted Garth's offer of hospitality. 'I'd like to go straight to the airport,' he said in his precise voice. 'No, don't drive me. I prefer a taxi. I expect your pilot to be waiting for me.'

'He will be,' Garth assured him.

'Not a charming character,' Miss McGeorge said when Wakeham had gone. 'But he's a genius at his job. You gave Barker the best possible chance.'

'But it's not a good chance, is it?' Garth asked.

'I'm afraid not. His age is still against him.'

Before being taken home the children begged to be allowed to say goodnight to Barker. Faye was reluctant, but Garth took their side.

'I'm afraid they'll be upset if they see him attached to a lot of machinery,' she protested.

'Not as upset as they'll be if he dies without them seeing him,' Garth said. And she realized he was right.

Like shadows they crept into the dimly lit room where he lay. As Faye had feared he was attached to drips and monitors, but both children simply ignored the machinery. They came close to Barker lying on the table, completely motionless except for the rise and fall of his breathing, and took it in turns to lift one of his floppy ears and whisper.

'I told him I loved him, so he's got to get well,' Cindy confided to her parents. 'But you must tell him too, so that he'll know we all need him.'

Faye murmured something loving into Barker's ear. But the really astonishing sight was Garth leaning down to say, 'Hang in there, boy. I've got a bone waiting for you at home like you wouldn't believe!'

'He heard you,' Cindy breathed. 'His nose twitched when you said "bone".'

'Darling, he's deeply unconscious,' Faye said.

'His nose twitched,' Garth said firmly. 'We saw it, didn't we?' He appealed to Adrian, who nodded.

They all crept out, pausing in the doorway for one more look at their friend who lay so silent and still.

By now it was long after midnight and the children could hardly keep their eyes open. Faye and Garth settled them gently in the back of the car and drove home. Nancy had gone ahead and was waiting to help put Cindy and Adrian to bed.

Faye went into the kitchen to make some tea. But as she reached out to the kettle she saw Barker's biscuits lying there, where she'd left them in the last moment before the nightmare began. The two red ones were still set apart, so that he could have them first. Perhaps he would never want them now. Suddenly unable to bear the sight, she rushed out of the kitchen and upstairs.

In her own room she was free to give way to her emotions. She left the light off and went to stand at the window, overlooking the spot where Barker had collapsed. She couldn't tear her eyes away from it and barely heard the click as Garth entered. He came close and touched her uncertainly on the shoulder.

'Faye,' he said quietly. 'Please—'

'It was down there,' she said huskily. 'They were playing ball and suddenly he made a different sound. Cindy called me and when I ran out he was lying stretched out on the ground—right there.'

'Hush!' he said, taking her into his arms. But she couldn't stop. The fear and grief of the day had caught up and overwhelmed her.

'He lay so still,' she choked. 'He's always been so full of life—into everything, and—and suddenly—he just didn't move—'

'Come away,' he said, drawing her away from the window.

'Suppose he never moves again—'

'Don't,' he begged her. 'You can't blame me more than I blame myself.'

'No, no, I didn't mean that— It's just that—he's one of the family and—I love him so much.'

'I know,' he said wryly. 'So do I.' He pressed her gently down on a small sofa and sat beside her. 'Take this,' he said, putting a glass into her hand. 'It's brandy. I brought it up because we both need one.'

She sipped it, and blew her nose. 'It's such a short time we've had Barker,' she said. 'Yet I can't imagine doing without him.'

'Perhaps we won't have to.' Garth drank some brandy and tried to steady himself. He'd skipped breakfast to make some final notes for his meeting and since then the only thing he'd had was Kendall's coffee. Now tension and an empty stomach were making him light-headed. It was hardly possible that he could be sitting here with Faye, talking like this in the darkness. At the same time, it seemed perfectly natural.

Faye was in no better state. Unlike Garth, she'd had

breakfast, and later a sandwich at the surgery. But she was exhausted and glad of the brandy.

'Dry your eyes,' he commanded, dabbing her face with his clean handkerchief. 'We've got to be positive about this. We've won so far and we're going to win in the end.'

'Are you sure?' He sounded so confident that she began to relax.

'Completely sure,' he said firmly. 'Barker's a fighter. He never gives up. Have you ever known him give up when there was something he wanted? Titbits, the best chair, making you stop work to throw his ball? Anything?'

'No,' she conceded. The authority in Garth's voice was almost hypnotic. He'd achieved so much today and it was suddenly easy to believe that he could order everything just as he wanted.

'You're right, he won't give up.' She managed a wonky smile. 'Stupid mutt. Always in the way—'

'Greedy, noisy, clumsy,' Garth supplied. 'Greedy.'

'You said greedy before,' she reminded him.

'However many times I said it, it would still be true. And dirty. Paws like plates, always covered in mud. Unscrupulous.' He hunted for something else. 'Greedy.'

'Scheming,' she supplied. 'Devious. He'd sell his grandmother for a titbit.'

'Dimwitted. Awkward.'

'And greedy.'

'Unreliable.'

'Not unreliable,' Faye protested. 'You could always rely on him to do the wrong thing.'

'That's true. Offend your neighbours, burgle your house, scratch your car—'

Faye broke down again. 'Oh, Garth, he will be all right, won't he? He's got to be.'

He put his arms around her and held her tightly, murmuring, 'It's all going to be fine. We couldn't go through all this for nothing.'

'You were wonderful getting Wakeham to come over.'

'Mr Fixit! That's me!'

'No, I'm serious. It meant so much to the children that you pulled out all the stops.'

'Only to the children?'

'Well, to me too, of course.'

'Yes, of course,' he said with a faint sigh. 'But I got it all the wrong way around, didn't I? If I'd listened to you in the first place—'

'Don't brood about that for ever. I heard what Cindy said to you tonight. She was right. They had him, even if just for a little while. Cindy's a very wise little person.'

'She's wonderful, isn't she? Just recently I've realized how like you she is. All heart. It worries me, because it makes her so vulnerable—mostly to me, at the moment.'

'Yes, she is. But at least you know. You can protect her.'

'Maybe I'm not so good at that. When you were—'

'What?' she asked, for he'd stopped, as if reluctant to say more.

'When we met—you were such a little thing, so delicate and young. You knew nothing about the world. I wanted to protect you from every wind that blew.'

'But I grew up,' she reminded him. 'And then you didn't know what to say to me any more.'

'Maybe I didn't want you to grow up,' he agreed. 'We were so happy then. I didn't want to let any part of it go. Besides, I thought you wanted me to be the strong one, and look after you. You said something once—'

'What did I say?'

'It was the week before Adrian was born and I'd just lost my job. Things looked about as black as they could be. I felt such a failure. Do you remember what you said?'

'Not the exact words, but I know I tried to tell you that I had confidence in you.'

'You said, "Don't worry. I know you'll make everything right." For a moment I was so scared at the trust you were putting in me. Then I knew I had to justify that trust, never trouble you with the burdens, but just make everything right for you—as you wanted me too.'

'But Garth,' she whispered in dismay. 'I was only trying to say that I believed in you, not that you should bear everything alone. I wanted to share all your troubles, but you started hiding them from me.'

'That's why.'

Light dawned on her. 'That time you nearly lost the builder's yard and you only just managed to save it—I didn't know about that until years later.'

'You weren't supposed to find out, ever. I was trying to make everything perfect for you, as a sort of thank-you.'

'Thank-you—for what?'

'For marrying me. I was so grateful. On our wedding day—' He stopped with an awkward laugh.

'Tell me,' she said eagerly. 'Don't stop now.'

'You were five minutes late at the church and I nearly went crazy. I thought you'd taken fright and weren't coming.'

'Why should I take fright?'

'Well, you didn't really want to marry me, did you?'

he said heavily. 'It was only because I made you pregnant.'

'But Garth—'

'I always knew, you see. You were so young. You wanted to laugh and have fun like other girls, and you had every right to. And because of me you ended up tied down, surrounded by a flat full of nappies. Oh, you never complained. You were very sweet about it. But it was always there between us, that I'd stolen your youth. I tried to give you everything to make up for it, but it was no good. I never really got it right, did I?'

Faye stared at him. 'You—*wanted* to marry me?'

'But you knew that. I did everything to get that ring on your finger.'

'Garth, I swear I didn't know. I thought I'd trapped you into marriage.'

'I never said you had.'

'No, but—you never mentioned marriage until then.'

'I didn't dare in case I frightened you off. When you told me about the baby I was thrilled because it was an excuse to make you marry me. I know I practically bullied you into it—telling you instead of asking you. But I was scared to ask in case you said no.' He gave an awkward laugh. 'You know what I'm like when I want something. I tend to grab. I grabbed you before you slipped through my fingers. I thought I'd won but I paid for it, because I was never certain of you afterwards.'

They stared at each other, with the truth between them for the first time.

'I never knew,' she whispered.

'Nor did I. Oh, Faye, what fools we were! All those years— Why did we throw them away?'

She shook her head, dumb with sadness.

'We might have had so much,' he said, 'and we missed our chance.'

'But we still had more happiness than many people have. Things went wrong, but at the start—'

'Yes,' he said heavily, 'we'll always have those memories. And we'll always know that it might have been better still if I hadn't been blind.' He sank his head on his hands.

Faye put her arms about him, overwhelmed by tenderness. 'It wasn't all your fault,' she murmured. 'We lost each other because we both made mistakes.'

He raised his face to her and she took it between her hands to kiss it gently. At first he did nothing, keeping perfectly still and letting her kisses fall on him like sweet balm. As he felt their loving message, the pain and tension seemed to fall away from him and he clung to her.

She wrapped her arms about him, finding again the vulnerable boy she'd fallen in love with. When she laid her lips softly on his, she felt his instant response.

'We might have had everything,' he whispered.

'Hush.' She kissed him to silence. 'We can still have everything, just for tonight.'

The last time they'd lain together in her bed it had been a union of bodies. Now it was a union of hearts. It was she who led the way, drawing him on at every step. Nothing mattered but consoling his pain

He clung to her in need as well as passion, savouring the warmth of her skin against his, losing himself in her bounty. Sometimes he seemed hesitant, but she offered him all of herself with a loving tenderness that enfolded him and he felt a man again, because this woman loved him.

She'd promised him everything, and she gave him everything. It might, as she'd said, be only for this one night, but they would have this memory in the years to come. Perhaps they would be lonely years, but the moment when their hearts and souls were one again would never entirely leave them.

In the darkness, his face pressed to her sweet-smelling body, it was easy for Garth to see that she, and she only, had given the world a meaning. He'd thrown it all away but she gave it back to him out of a generous spirit. He was more than making love to her. He was seeking refuge in her. And now he understood that this was how it had always been.

As the first light came through the curtains Garth rose from Faye's bed. He stood looking down at her, sleeping as peacefully as a child, then turned away as though the sight smote him. He was hearing Cindy's voice the night before, knowing that her words were wise and generous yet not wanting to face it.

He bent and kissed his sleeping wife, softly, not to disturb her. His heart was heavy as he slipped quietly out of the room.

His children were up before him, standing watching the hall telephone.

'Can we ring the vet and ask now?' Adrian demanded.

'It's too early. They'll still be checking him. But if Barker— If anything had gone wrong in the night, they'd have called us by now.'

'Perhaps they haven't got our number?' Cindy suggested.

'They've got it, I promise.'

They drifted out into the garden. Cindy found the ball Barker had dropped, scrubbed it with her hanky and put it back in exactly the same place on the grass. Garth wondered if it would ever be needed again. He watched

Cindy with anxious eyes, struck by her strength and self-control; surely too much for a child?

Faye came down and he greeted her with a distant smile, but didn't go to her. The resolution he'd made in the early hours hung heavily on him and he was sorely tempted to abandon it. But he stopped himself. It had taken him too long to decide on the right thing. But he knew now what it was and there would be no weakening.

'Why don't you just call the vet?' Faye asked Garth softly.

'They'll call us when they're ready.'

She stared. Garth had never been afraid to barge in and demand answers. And then she understood. He was scared. Everything hung on what they would learn this morning. Tenderly she squeezed his hand.

The phone rang.

Everyone jumped. Nobody moved. Then Garth forced himself to answer. The silence seemed to last a long time, before he said, 'Thank you for telling me.'

He laid down the receiver very carefully, as though delaying the moment when he must speak. Then he grinned at his family and said, 'Barker's eating a hearty breakfast.'

Barker was home in a week. He still needed care, but nobody could have done the job more thoroughly than his family. Cindy appointed herself head nurse, with Adrian to assist her. Nancy deputized while they were at school, with Faye and Garth permitted to visit the invalid with appropriate gifts, all of which were consumed in seconds.

Cindy was fast growing up, becoming more firmly in charge and more like her father. When she decided the patient was gorging himself and not getting enough exercise, she read him a stern lecture and forbade all further titbits. Barker began to look harassed.

'Don't worry, old fellow,' Garth reassured him after three weeks of this. 'I've got a special present for you tomorrow; one you're going to love, and "Matron" won't be able to lock it away.'

He was home early the next evening, looking as though he was concealing a secret.

'Where are the kids?' he asked Faye quietly.

'Playing with Barker in the garden.'

'Good. I've brought someone home with me and I want you to be the first to meet her.'

'Her?'

'Wait here,' he said, with a touch of mischief.

When he returned a moment later, Faye's eyes widened at the sight of his companion.

'Her name is Peaches,' Garth said.

Peaches was a really lovely St Bernard with liquid eyes and a melting expression.

'She's a year old,' Garth explained, 'and her owner had to rehome her because she's a bit of a handful. But she's—er—' he paused, seeking for words '—just ready to become a bride,' he finished delicately. 'I thought Barker would like her.'

From outside came a squeal and the sound of thundering paws. Barker appeared, followed by the children, and stopped dead in the doorway, his gaze riveted by the vision of beauty before him. Peaches gazed back. Their eyes met across a crowded room. Cindy and Adrian regarded the scene with awe.

'He just suddenly dropped the ball and dashed inside,' Cindy said. 'It was like he knew...'

'I think he did,' Garth agreed. 'Meet Peaches. She's come to keep Barker company while you're at school.'

The children made a fuss of Peaches, who responded amiably, but her languishing gaze constantly travelled towards Barker, whose virile form had clearly made a deep impression.

'All they needed was a swelling orchestra,' Garth said with a grin when he was alone with Faye later.

'What made you do it?' she asked.

'Barker's still an old dog and he's getting older. We can't put the sad day off for ever. But this way, we'll never really lose him. Why are you surprised? I told you I'd do something.'

'But I thought you were simply going to get another dog.'

'And I have. But just any dog wouldn't do. It's Barker who matters. With Peaches's help, he'll leave something of himself behind.'

CHAPTER TWELVE

To the amusement of the whole family, Barker's passion for Peaches developed into slavish infatuation. She was a domestic tyrant, blowing hot and cold; one day allowing him to smooch her lovingly, the next, growling him away. But nothing could cool Barker's chivalrous devotion and in the presence of his beloved he was reduced to a state of doting idiocy.

'Poor Barker,' Cindy consoled him. 'You're a henpecked husband.'

'And when his pups are born he'll be a henpecked father,' Garth had observed, tweaking her hair. 'Like me.'

Four weeks after their first meeting, Miss McGeorge had confirmed that Peaches was pregnant. Barker strutted about, every inch the proud father, and Cindy and Adrian began to squabble about names for the pups.

The tenth anniversary was growing closer. Faye had relented about letting the children take part, because she was grateful to Garth for putting them before business, even at the cost of the Newcastle contract. He never complained, nor even mentioned the matter, and Faye only knew for sure that he'd lost it when Mary told her. It was like the old days, when he hadn't confided in her.

There was something else he'd kept to himself, which hurt far more. Kendall had telephoned to ask how she was and she'd told him about Barker's crisis. That was how she learned that Garth had sought his help in getting James Wakeham. At first she was delighted. This was exactly the kind of generous act she'd dreamed of seeing him make. But joy was succeeded by sadness at the way he'd excluded her. He'd done it for Cindy and although he could have won his wife's approval, it seemed that he hadn't bothered.

Then Kendall said something else that astonished her.

'It's nice that you're still speaking to me.'

'Why shouldn't I be?'

'I imagine Garth told you all about Jane.'

'She's your new secretary, isn't she? Why should Garth have mentioned her?'

'You mean he didn't? That's amazing. I thought he'd have made the most of it.'

'Kendall, I don't know what you're talking about.'

'Jane works late for me sometimes, and we have a meal together, and—and so on. She was here the night Garth came. Look, I was just a bit lonely for you. It doesn't have to mean anything if we don't let it.'

As Faye understood what he was really saying she waited for the surge of pain it should have brought her. But there was nothing. Kendall had found someone else to flatter his vanity. He was a kindly enough man in his way, but he liked being the centre of attention. What had followed was inevitable and perhaps she had always secretly guessed it.

'Tell me, Kendall,' she said, 'does Jane ever forget to watch you on television?'

'Well—no,' he admitted sheepishly.

'Then you should marry her without delay. And I'll dance at your wedding. Goodbye, my dear.'

She hung up, her thoughts in turmoil. It was ironic to remember now how she'd once said about Garth, 'I wouldn't put it past him to have my replacement lined up to massage his ego, just in case.' But it was Kendall

who'd done exactly that and Garth who had remained true.

But no longer, it seemed. He'd known that Kendall
had found someone else, yet he hadn't tried to make any
use of it.

If he'd truly wanted me, she thought despondently,
he'd have told me about this, hoping to turn me against
Kendall.

But he'd preferred to leave Kendall's image untar-
nished. There was surely only one explanation. When
the anniversary gala was over, he would be finished with
her.

Cindy was looking forward to the banquet, and was
thrilled with her new party frock. Adrian eyed his formal
clothes askance and muttered, 'Do I have to, Mum?'

She'd bought the kind of glamorous dress Garth
wanted, a black, figure-hugging creation that would be
a good background for diamonds. The children were
loud in their admiration, and Faye was agreeably surprised by her own appearance.

Garth, too, approved. At least, he nodded and said,
'Good. You'll look just right.'

She'd smiled to cover her disappointment that he
showed so little warmth. But what had she expected?
Since the night of their loving she'd hoped for so much
and been granted so little. She'd had a glimpse of Garth
as he'd once been, as she longed for him to be again.
But he'd retired behind a barrier from which he emerged
only for his children.

Since Kendall's revelation, she knew that Garth was
simply biding his time until their final break-up. And,
with terrible irony, this happened just as she faced the
fact that she'd never really stopped loving her husband.

But he'd reclaimed her only out of pride, and lost

interest when she was his for the asking. Sometimes she would surprise him with a strange look in his eyes, as though he was planning the next move. Perhaps he would offer her money to move out and let him keep the children?

She flinched at the thought of leaving them, but wouldn't it be kinder to let them stay here, with the father they adored?

Only a little while ago she'd seemed to have almost everything. Now she was on the verge of losing everything. And worst of all was the thought that Garth might have planned this from the start.

On the evening of the banquet Faye let Cindy help her on with the black velvet evening cloak, with its white satin lining.

'You look gorgeous, Mummy,' the little girl breathed.

'Thank you, darling.'

'Doesn't she?' Cindy demanded of her brother.

But he was covered in nine-year-old male confusion and could only mumble, 'Yeah.'

Cindy ran off to inform her father that Mummy looked simply *gorgeous*. Adrian regarded his mother awkwardly for a moment, before pecking her cheek and offering her his arm.

'Thank you, kind sir,' she teased.

Garth's eyes never left her as she made her entrance down the staircase. He looked satisfied. There was something else in his expression, too, but she couldn't read him any more.

'You look gorgeous,' he said as she reached the bottom. 'I've been instructed that that's the right word,' he added with a teasing glance at Cindy, who was watching him severely. The little girl smiled and relaxed, evidently feeling that he was doing the proper thing. Faye couldn't help smiling too, at the perfect understanding between father and child. She put her head up and assumed a dazzling smile as she offered Garth her hand and let him lead her to the waiting car.

The reception was being held at the Ritz. They travelled there in a stretch limo, with the children sitting up ahead, which gave the two adults the illusion of privacy. Faye had a curious feeling that Garth was nervous, yet his words sounded confident.

'The place will be packed tonight. We didn't get a single refusal.'

'I shouldn't think they dared,' she quipped. 'Not once you'd made your wishes known. Another huge success for Garth Clayton. Isn't that how it goes?'

'Some successes matter more than others,' he observed in a strange voice. But he was looking out of the window, not at her.

As he'd predicted, every seat was taken. When the family walked in, the crowd rose in applause. The lights were too brilliant for her to discern much but she'd been through a rehearsal and knew that models of the houses were placed around the great ballroom, and everywhere there was silver glitter the colour of diamonds.

Afterwards she couldn't remember details. There was a perfectly prepared and served meal, with excellent wines. Speeches followed. Faye heard none of them, until Garth rose to his feet.

She was on edge in case he spoke about their marriage, twisting the facts into a publicity presentation. But to her relief he began talking about the start of his business.

'It was a builder's yard with a door that didn't lock properly. Not that it mattered much, because there was nothing in there worth stealing,' he announced, to laughter. 'You never saw a shabbier place, but I called it Clayton Properties.

'My wife and I had two tin plates to eat off, and we were so poor that I used to take one to work for lunch, to save buying a third. Once I forgot to take it home at night, so we shared hers.'

Yes, it had happened like that, she thought. They'd squabbled over that plate, each wanting the other to have it first. In the end, they'd eaten together and Garth had marked the occasion by scratching two entwined hearts in the centre. She'd wanted to keep the plate, but Garth had taken it to the yard, and lost it.

'Since then, Clayton Properties has grown and grown again,' he said. 'But I still fondly remember that first little yard, how proud I was of it and how proud my wife was of me. She never saw it as a dump. She thought that now I'd entered the market the rest of them might as well give up.' There was friendly laughter and a smattering of applause, then he went on. 'And because she believed that, I began to believe it. I went on because I had to justify her faith in me. And I found I could take giant strides I'd never dreamed of.

'I did things I was scared to do, because I couldn't risk Faye finding out that I had feet of clay. Of course, she knew that all the time, but she didn't let on because she didn't want *me* to find out.'

This time the laughter was loud, with a warm, friendly tone. Everyone knew that this was an excellent speech, striking just the right note for the occasion.

But Faye never thought of it like that. She was listening intently to the man she loved, breathless with hope.

'Clayton Properties has been as much her creation as

mine. And that's why it's right that I should honour her tonight, on our tenth wedding anniversary.'

He took her hand to raise her up, and opened the black box in front of him. A rivière of diamonds glittered inside. The crowd rose in thunderous applause as he fitted the lavish jewels about her neck. Faye hardly heard them. She was looking into Garth's smiling eyes, feeling the warm touch of his hands on her neck. Everything was coming right at last. He'd only been waiting for tonight.

In her joy she was able to pose for the photographs with a truly radiant smile. It was going to be all right. Tonight, when the children had gone to bed, he would tell her what was in his heart and they would find each other again. She could have sung with happiness.

It seemed an eternity until the party broke up, but at last they were all moving towards the door. Her hand was tucked in Garth's arm. She could see the car waiting for them through the great entrance. In a few minutes they would be inside it, perhaps in each other's arms. Cindy and Adrian would giggle, but they were welcome.

Suddenly Garth tensed and stopped. He seemed awkward. 'Faye, I should have told you this before. Something came up this afternoon.'

She stared at him in disbelief. Oh, this couldn't be happening again!

'I was going to France in a few days, but I've had a call to say they need me earlier. I've got to leave for the airport straight away.'

'You're not even coming home with us?' she gasped.

'When you get there you'll understand. Please believe me— This is best.'

Cindy and Adrian came beside them, looking up with silent questions as they sensed the changed atmosphere.

'Daddy has to go to France on urgent business,' Faye said, hardly knowing what she was saying.

'You mean you're not coming home with us?' Adrian asked.

'Not just for the— Cindy, what have you got there? It's not a doggy bag, is it?'

Cindy guiltily produced not one bag but two.

'There's Peaches as well,' she explained, 'and she's eating for three or four or five or—'

Something strange seemed to happen to Garth. He closed his eyes and for a moment Faye could have sworn that his lips were shaking, as though he was on the verge of tears. But that didn't make sense.

'I just hope you've got enough for her,' he said at last. He dropped to one knee and put an arm around each child, hugging them tightly. ''Bye kids,' he said huskily. 'Be good.'

There was a mysterious undercurrent in his voice. Faye stared at him, trying desperately to understand.

'I'll take you to the car,' he said.

'Garth—' she cried. She was suddenly scared.

'Faye.' He said her name so softly that she barely heard. He reached out and touched her cheek and there was something in his eyes that broke her heart. Abruptly he seized her and pulled her hard against him, burying his face in her hair. Then, just as quickly, he thrust her from him.

'Goodbye, Faye,' he said hoarsely, and turned back inside.

It was all over, she thought, as she was borne home. The distance he'd set between them recently had been a warning. Tonight he'd played his part so beautifully that she had been taken in.

In her heart she knew what she would find when she

reached home. There would be a letter announcing that everything was over between them. He'd had all he needed of her.

Nancy was waiting up to put the children to bed. She didn't comment on Garth's absence. Nor did she look at Faye as she said, 'There's something in your room. He told me to put it there when you'd all left.'

The envelope was lying on her pillow, her name written in Garth's bold hand. With trembling hands she opened it, and read:

My darling Faye,

This is the hardest letter I've ever had to write, because it's a goodbye, and that's a word I swore I'd never say to you. I love you so much. I never stopped loving you for a moment, but I killed your love and couldn't get it back.

Once it seemed easy. I thought I had the power to force you back to me. I managed it in one way, but the more we were together, the more I realized that your heart had slipped away. Perhaps I was never the man for you. I only seem to make you unhappy.

There's something you must know. When Barker was dying I went to Kendall Haines and begged him to use his influence to get James Wakeham. I meant to tell you next day, when things were calmer. But I never did, because that night something happened that changed everything.

Earlier Cindy had asked me to have Barker put to sleep. She said, 'If you love someone, you've got to let them go, if it's best for them.'

I didn't see the implications for us at first, but then you loved me with such sweetness and warmth that I knew only the best was good enough for you. And the best is to escape from me. You once said that nobody could be happy with me. And you were right.

So I never told you about approaching Haines, because it might have made it harder for you to leave me. I didn't want you staying because I'd 'earned' it, but only because you loved me. And you're safer not loving me.

I learned something about Haines too, that night. He's not the man you think he is. He co-opted his secretary to fill your place without much loss of time. I wasn't sure whether to tell you, or whether it would be interfering in your life. You might not even have believed me. But now I won't be here, you must know the truth. Don't marry him, my darling. Wait for someone else who's better than both of us.

It's taken me too long to learn wisdom from my daughter, but I know now that the truest way I can show my love is by letting you go.

I won't be returning to Elm Ridge. I want you and Cindy and Adrian to stay there. After the divorce I'd like to see the children often, but I promise never to trouble you.

It's the tenth anniversary of our wedding, and I've showered you with diamonds, as the firm expected me to. But my real anniversary gift is something else. You'll find it in a parcel next to this letter. I wonder if you'll recognize it. If so, I like to think it will still mean something to you.

Goodbye, my dearest. I love you so very much.

Garth.

She had to read the letter twice. There was a blank look in her eyes as the incredible truth came home to her, and she let out her breath in a long sigh.

'You fool,' she murmured. 'How could you be so blind?'

But did she mean him, or herself? She honestly couldn't have said.

The little parcel lay on the bed. It was plainly wrapped in brown paper and carried no tag. She was almost afraid as she opened it.

Inside she found the tin plate Garth had mentioned in his speech, with the two entwined hearts scratched in the centre. Tears began to roll down her cheeks. She'd thought he'd tossed those early days aside contemptuously, but he'd remembered as vividly as herself. Despite his brash exterior, he'd secretly treasured this memento all these years. Now it had a slightly forlorn, abandoned look.

Her happiness was almost too great to be borne, but her tears still flowed. They were for him, going away, believing that she didn't love him. How could it end this way? How could two people who loved each other so much manage to lose each other?

Then her head went up. She wasn't going to give in without a fight. With trembling fingers she dialled the airport number and was put through to Bill's little cubby hole.

'Bill, it's Faye. Is Garth there yet?'

'No, but he's due at any moment. Our take-off slot is in half an hour.'

'He mustn't go. Bill, you've got to stop him.'

'Stop him?' Bill sounded aghast. 'You mean you want me to give him a message from you?'

'No, there's no message.' Garth could be stubborn when he'd made a decision. If he knew she was following him, he would leave all the faster.

'Then I can't delay him,' Bill protested.

'You simply must. Develop a mechanical breakdown, chuck a spanner in the engine. *Anything*. But stop him leaving.'

Bill's voice became plaintive. 'Mrs Clayton, have you any idea what's it's like being caught between the two of you? You're as bad as each other.'

'I'm sure you can manage to think of something, Bill.' She found Nancy. 'I've got to go out.'

'At this hour? Where are you going?'

'To save my marriage,' Faye said and hurried outside.

She was a careful driver, who disliked driving at night. But when she saw the road clear ahead she put down her foot. She was relying on Bill to hold Garth up, but how long could he manage it?

Half an hour kept throbbing through her brain. Half an hour and it might all be too late. It was no use to argue that she could contact him later. The moment was now and if she missed it, it would have gone forever.

'Wait for me, Garth,' she murmured as she drove. 'Don't take off. Listen to me calling you. Listen to my love, and turn back to me.'

At last she could see the lights in the distance which told her she was nearing the airport. Luckily the security guard recognized her.

'Has my husband taken off yet?' she asked in terrible fear.

'Just about to.'

'No,' she cried frantically.

As the hangar came into sight she could just make out two figures walking towards the plane. One of them was Bill, who seemed to be arguing frantically. The other was Garth. With the wind in her direction Faye could hear him say, 'That's enough, Bill. Now let's get on, I'm in a hurry.'

'Garth!' she called. *'Garth!'*

But the wind whipped her words away and she knew he hadn't heard her. She'd reached the steel barrier, beyond which she couldn't take the car. Wildly she jumped out, pushed through a small gap in the barrier and began to run as if her life depended on it.

'Garth!' she screamed.

At last he heard her. She saw him stop, but he didn't turn. It was as if he feared an hallucination so sweet that it must be resisted.

She called his name again and this time he looked round, his face torn between hope and despair as he saw her.

'I love you,' she called. 'We all love you. Don't leave us.'

He began to run back to her, but at the last moment something stopped him. 'Faye, did you get my letter?' he called.

'Yes, I read it, and you've got everything wrong. We love you. Don't you understand? We love you.'

'We?'

'*I* love you. I always have. It broke my heart to leave you two years ago, but I thought you didn't love me.' She drew nearer to him. 'After the night we came together I was sure everything would be all right, but then you pushed me away.'

'I was afraid. I thought I'd taken advantage of you— You were so unhappy— The brandy— Maybe you didn't know what you were doing—'

'One glass! What do you think I am? Some brainless little girl who needs her hand held? Maybe I *was* when I married you, but not now. Garth, how dare you make this decision without consulting me. I knew exactly what

I was doing that night. I was loving you, and that's what
I meant to do.'

'*Faye*—'

'And I'm going to go on doing it. I'm sure about that
too. You're not going to France tonight.'

'Aren't I?'

'No, because this time I'm making the decision. And
my decision is that you're coming home with me, and
we're going to awaken our children and tell them that
our marriage is on again, and this time it's for ever.'

He came close and searched her face. 'Is that what
we're going to do?' he asked breathlessly.

'That's exactly what we're going to do. Any arguments?'

He seized her in his arms.

'Not from me,' he said joyfully. 'Let's go and do it
right now.'

❧ Harlequin Romance®

Everyone has special occasions in their life.
Maybe an engagement, a wedding, an anniversary, the
birth of a baby. Or even a personal milestone—a
thirtieth or fortieth birthday!

**These are times of celebration and excitement,
and we're delighted to bring you
a special new series called...**

One special occasion— that changes your life forever!

We'll be featuring one terrific book each month,
starting in May 1998...

May 1998—BABY IN A MILLION
by Rebecca Winters (#3503)
June 1998—BERESFORD'S BRIDE
by Margaret Way (#3507)
July 1998—BIRTHDAY BRIDE
by Jessica Hart (#3511)
August 1998—THE DIAMOND DAD
by Lucy Gordon (#3515)

Look in the back pages of any *Big Event* book to find
out how to receive a set of sparkling wineglasses.

Available wherever Harlequin books are sold.

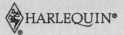

Not The Same Old Story!

HARLEQUIN PRESENTS®
Exciting, glamorous romance stories that take readers around the world.

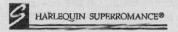
Sparkling, fresh and tender love stories that bring you pure romance.

Bold and adventurous— Temptation is strong women, bad boys, great sex!

HARLEQUIN SUPERROMANCE®
Provocative and realistic stories that celebrate life and love.

Contemporary fairy tales—where anything is possible and where dreams come true.

HARLEQUIN INTRIGUE®
Heart-stopping, suspenseful adventures that combine the best of romance and mystery.

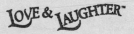
Humorous and romantic stories that capture the lighter side of love.

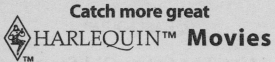 

HARLEQUIN 🂱 PRESENTS®

Everyone has special occasions in their life—an engagement, a wedding, an anniversary…or maybe the birth of a baby.

These are times of celebration and excitement, and we're delighted to bring you a special new series called…

One special occasion—that changes your life forever!

Celebrate *The Big Event!* with great books by some of your favorite authors:

September 1998—BRIDE FOR A YEAR
by Kathryn Ross (#1981)

October 1998—MARRIAGE MAKE UP
by Penny Jordan (#1983)

November 1998—RUNAWAY FIANCÉE
by Sally Wentworth (#1992)

December 1998—BABY INCLUDED!
by Mary Lyons (#1997)

Look in the back pages of any *Big Event* book to find out how to receive a set of sparkling wineglasses.

Available wherever Harlequin books are sold.

🂱 HARLEQUIN®
Makes any time special ™

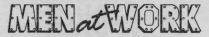

MEN at WORK

All work and no play?
Not these men!

July 1998
MACKENZIE'S LADY by Dallas Schulze
Undercover agent Mackenzie Donahue's
lazy smile and deep blue eyes were his best
weapons. But after rescuing—and kissing!—
damsel in distress Holly Reynolds, how could
he betray her by spying on her brother?

August 1998
MISS LIZ'S PASSION by Sherryl Woods
Todd Lewis could put up a building with ease,
but quailed at the sight of a classroom! Still,
Liz Gentry, his son's teacher, was no battle-ax,
and soon Todd started planning some
extracurricular activities of his own....

September 1998
A CLASSIC ENCOUNTER
by Emilie Richards
Doctor Chris Matthews was intelligent, sexy
and *very* good with his hands—which made
him all the more dangerous to single mom
Lizette St. Hilaire. So how long could she
resist Chris's special brand of TLC?

Available at your favorite retail outlet!

MEN AT WORK™

Toast the special events in your life with Harlequin Romance®!

With the purchase of *two* Harlequin Romance® BIG EVENT books, you can send for two sparkling plum-colored Wine Glasses, retail value $19.95!

To complete your set, see details inside any Harlequin Presents® title in September 1998!

ACT NOW TO COLLECT TWO FREE WINE GLASSES!

Fill in the official proof-of-purchase coupon below and send it, plus $2.99 U.S./$3.99 CAN. for postage and handling (check or money order—please do not send cash), to Harlequin Books: In the U.S.: 3010 Walden Avenue, P.O. Box 9077, Buffalo, NY 14269-9077; In Canada: P.O. Box 609, Fort Erie, Ontario L2A 5X3. Please allow 4-6 weeks for delivery. Order your set of wine glasses now! Quantities are limited. Offer for the Plum Wine Glasses expires December 31, 1998.

Harlequin Romance®—The Big Event!

OFFICIAL PROOF OF PURCHASE

"Please send me my TWO Wine Glasses"

Name: _____

Address: _____

City: _____

State/Prov.: _____ Zip/Postal Code: _____

Account Number: _____ 097 KGS CSA6 193-3

HRBEPOP

HARLEQUIN®
Makes any time special ™